An Alien H[e]
With My Homework!

Lisa Smith and Kimberly Arcand

An Alien Helped Me with My Homework. Copyright © 2020 Lisa Smith and Kimberly Arcand. Produced and printed by Stillwater River Publications. All rights reserved. Written and produced in the United States of America. This book may not be reproduced or sold in any form without the expressed, written permission of the authors and publisher.

Visit our website at www.StillwaterPress.com for more information.

First Stillwater River Publications Edition

Library of Congress Control Number 2019920864

ISBN-13: 978-1-950-33987-7

1 2 3 4 5 6 7 8 9

Written by Lisa Smith and Kimberly Arcand
Cover and art by Christopher Hilaire
Published by Stillwater River Publications, Pawtucket, RI, USA.

For our children and granddaughters,
the *real* Jackson, Clara, Daria, Olenna, Gwendolyn, and Elodie.
Your stars shine brightest in our skies!

N K

Contents

Chapter 1 – My Big Sister Is A Pain

"I HATE HER!" Jackson Bishop slammed the back door into his kitchen.
"I HATE HER! I HATE HER! I HATE HER!"

"Hold it right there Jackson!" his mother, Clara, said. "You know we don't talk like that in this house. What has you so fired up?"

"It's my teacher," Jax explained. "I haaa... She's so annoying."

Clara sighed. "Why don't we sit down and you can tell me what happened?"

Jax sat down with his head in his hands. Clara sensed that this was a real problem, so she poured two glasses of milk and brought the cookie jar over to the table.

"Go ahead," she said. "I want all the details."

"Well," Jax said, "She ruined school break."

"Your entire holiday? How?"

"Mmphh ssh grrp..."

Clara interrupted, "How about swallowing that cookie first and then you can start from the beginning."

"OK," Jax said after taking a big gulp of milk to wash down the cookie. "She assigned a massive report and it's due the day we come back from break. It's *so* unfair!"

"That isn't what happened, Jackson, and you know it!" Gwen, Jackson's older sister, had joined them in the kitchen. Gwen was 13, two years older than Jackson, and as far as Jax was concerned, she should go far away and leave him alone. When

Gwen wasn't texting her BFF, Ellie, or asking for a ride to see her friends, she was a major-league snitch. About Jax. No matter how much their Mom explained to her that no one likes a tattletale, it felt like Gwen lived to get Jax in trouble.

Clara wanted to know what was going on, but she knew enough to sit quietly and just look at her two kids, one at a time, until one spilled the real story. It wasn't easy being a single mom. Ever since her husband had died last year, she had been trying to figure out how to be mom, dad, and everything in between for Jax and Gwen. This time, she didn't have to wait long. Gwen was the first to break the silence.

"Jax knew about that assignment two weeks ago," Gwen said. "Ellie's sister is in Jax's class, and she already has *her* project all done."

Clara looked at Jax and raised one eyebrow as if to say, "Well, your turn."

Jackson gave his sister a look and sighed. "Yeah. OK. But you want me to stay on the soccer team and we've had a lot of practices so we'll be ready for the big tournament."

"You know I don't like excuses, Jackson. And schoolwork always comes first." Inside, though, Clara knew that she had been encouraging Jax to stay on the soccer team. All the parents took turns helping at practices. Clara suspected that without his dad to encourage him and without her being able to make much time to help, Jax felt like he was on his own. It didn't help that he wasn't exactly the best player on the team. It had only been in the past month, when his best friend, Jefferson, offered to share his parents at practices, that Jackson had started to look forward to playing on the team again.

"Jeff hasn't done his project, either."

"That's the best you can do?" Gwen chimed in.

"Be quiet, Fish Fart Face!"

Fish Fart Face was what Jax and Jefferson called Gwen. They knew it really made her angry. When they *really* wanted to get to her, they made a "*FFFFFF*" sound in her direction. Not to be outdone, Gwen got back at them by calling them "The Presidents." Jackson and Jefferson secretly liked that, but they'd never let Gwen know or she might think of something else to call them that actually was annoying.

Clara would be very happy when Gwen and Jax stopped calling each other names, but right now, she wanted to get to the bottom of the immediate problem.

"Enough, and no name calling please. Gwen, why don't you go FaceTime Ellie? From your room. Jackson, don't move. Now, talk."

Jackson took a deep breath and explained, "We have to find three facts about outer space that surprised us and write about them."

"But that sounds like fun!" Clara said. "You love reading about space."

It was true. Jackson's room was full of posters and models of rockets. His ceiling was covered in stars that glowed in the dark. It was no secret that Jax wanted to be an astronaut, or work at NASA on something to do with distant stars and planets. When it was a clear night, he liked to gaze out of his window at the stars. When it was too cloudy to see anything in the night sky, he'd look at the glowing stars on the ceiling and imagine he was seeing them up close from a spaceship.

Jax looked at his mom and said, "That's just it, Mom. I don't know how I'm going to find something surprising. I'm stuck."

"Jax, hon, you can't possibly know everything there is to know about space. There's literally a whole Universe out there. It sounds more like you've been procrastinating—putting things off—and now you're going to have to work hard so you don't have this project hanging over you for the whole school break."

Then Clara added, "How about I help you make a plan to get started?"

"It's fine Mom. Thanks, but I'll do it. I just need to get online and find somewhere to start."

Jackson really appreciated that his mom rarely lost her temper, even when he and Gwen were acting up. He refilled his glass of milk and headed for his room to get started. Ollie, his big shaggy dog, followed him, tail wagging, hoping for some of the dog treats that Jax kept in a jar on his desk.

"Good boy, Ollie," Jax said as he gave him a treat and rubbed his head. "Well, what do you think? Let's see what's out there."

Jax closed his door, sat down at his desk, and turned on his laptop.

And that's when it all got very, *very* strange.

Chapter 2 – There's an Alien in My Laptop

Suddenly, Jax's room was plunged into darkness. He couldn't even see the stars that should have been glowing on his ceiling.

"Uh....," Jax whispered. "Ollie? Are you there, boy?"

Ollie gave a very quiet whimper and leaned up against Jackson's leg.

"Did I blow a fuse or something?"

But deep down, Jax didn't really think it was a blown fuse. It wasn't even 4pm and the Sun had been shining just seconds before. It should have been light outside his window. Instead, it was like his whole room had been sucked into a black hole or something.

Afraid to move but also afraid not to, Jackson slowly pushed his desk chair back and stood up, glad that his desk wasn't too far from the door to his room. He opened the door and stepped out into the familiar hallway leading to the kitchen. It was all bright and cheery, just as it should have been.

"Mom?" Jax called. "Can you check if there's a fuse that isn't right?"

His mom called back, "Why? What happened?"

"Oh, probably nothing. Just the light...on my d-desk...in my r-room...." Jax was stammering. He wasn't sure what to say. If he said that his laptop hadn't come on and his room had been plunged into darkness, his mom probably would think he was procrastinating again. Or worse, she might come walking into his own personal—and maybe even dangerous—black hole. Or whatever it was.

"Hang on. Give me a minute to get down to the basement to check," his mom said. A few seconds later, she called up from the basement, "All good down here. Make sure the bulb hasn't burned out, OK?"

"OK! Thanks." Jax called back as brightly as he could.

"You heard her, Ollie. We're going back in. Maybe I just imagined it. Maybe the laptop will be on and everything will be totally normal."

Ollie looked at Jax and turned his head to one side. If a dog could look doubtful, Ollie sure did. He also didn't move from where he was lying down in the hallway.

"Oh, come on. I'm not going back in there alone." Ollie stayed where he was.

"How about another treat?"

With those magic words, Ollie got up and followed Jax, but his tail was not doing its usual mile-a-minute wag.

Jax slowly opened the door to his room, but before it was halfway open, he could tell that the darkness was still there. Ollie tried to back up down the hallway, but Jax had a firm grip on his collar.

"I'm not going in there by myself!" he whispered to Ollie. "Don't be such a wimp!"

As Jax and Ollie entered the room, Jax whispered, "Dad? Is that you? Is someone here?" But no one answered him.

Not yet.

The blackness began to swirl and change. It no longer looked like a black hole. Instead, Jax felt like he was in the middle of a field of stars. Not like the stars on his ceiling, but real stars. They were everywhere, shining through the darkness.

Then a face began to appear on his laptop's screen.

It was a girl. At least Jax thought it was a girl, but she didn't look like any girl he'd ever seen. Her hair was pink and lavender and yellow. It was long, and it swirled around her head and behind her, almost filling the screen. There were sparkles in it, too, as if it had stars sprinkled through it. She had huge green eyes that looked more like they belonged on a cat than a person, and she had a small mouth, with red lips that widened into a smile as she looked right at Jackson.

"Uh…wow. Hello?" Jackson very hesitantly said. It sounded more like a question than a greeting.

"Hello!" The girl—or whatever it was—cheerfully replied. "I'm Zaria. What are you called?" she asked.

"I'm…Jackson, but most people call me Jax. Except when I'm in trouble." Jax had no idea why he said that, but he thought he had to say something.

"*Who are you?*" he asked Zaria. He didn't want to sound rude but he was pretty sure that this was no ordinary girl. And he had no idea what she was doing in his laptop…or at least on his laptop's screen.

Zaria laughed, and it sounded like all the stars that were still swirling around his room seemed to laugh, too. It was a light, twinkly sound, like the wind chime that hung from the back porch outside.

"I told you!" she said. "I'm Zaria."

"Noooo…I mean, who *are* you? I've never seen you around school or in my neighborhood. Are you new? Did you just move here? And how did you get on my laptop? What are those stars? And…."

"*Wait!*" Zaria held up a very slender arm with her hand facing him, palm out. "One question at a time, please."

Just as Jax was starting to think that Zaria sounded like Gwen when she tried to act like His Big Sister in Charge of Everything, what Zaria said next stopped him cold.

"I'm from the planet ZX55A, but we just call it Zix."

Chapter 3 – Zaria From Zix

Jax felt his eyes grow large and round. "The planet *what*?!"

"ZX55A. Zix for short. You know there is life on other planets, right?"

"Ummm…not for sure," Jax replied. "Until now. Hold on. If you're from another planet, how can you speak English?"

Zaria smiled. "Beings from Zix are…well…more advanced than you are on Earth. We can travel great distances and understand other beings."

"Can you understand Ollie, my dog?" Jax asked.

"Of course!" Zaria answered. She looked at Ollie. "Hello Ollie! You are very handsome. Is there anything you'd like me to tell Jax?"

Ollie made soft woofing sounds for about a minute. Jax kept looking at Ollie, then Zaria, then back to Ollie, then Zaria. He wouldn't have believed it if he weren't seeing it with his own eyes, but it really looked like Ollie was talking to Zaria. And Zaria, well, she was tilting her head and listening, just like Ollie did when Jax talked to him. When Ollie stopped, Jax looked at Zaria.

"What was all that about?" he asked.

"Ollie likes his name, doesn't like the cat next door, and most of all would appreciate a few treats," Zaria said.

Jax looked at Ollie. "REALLY?! The first time you can talk to me directly and all you can think about is your doggy stomach and getting more treats?!"

Ollie looked at him with what could only be described as a smile and Zaria laughed out loud.

"OK, boy, but this is your last treat for a while. Now it's *my* turn to talk to Zaria! So, Zaria, do you really look like that?"

"Not really," she replied. "Beings from Zix can take on different forms."

"You mean like a dragon? Or a tree?" Jax was thinking of how cool it would be to ask Zaria if she could come out of the laptop, change into a snake, and scare his sister.

"Sure, but we only change our form if there's a good reason. Like now."

Jax thought scaring Fish Fart Face would be a perfect reason. Instead, he asked, "What is your reason?"

But at that point, they were interrupted. Jax heard his mom calling.

"Jackson, are you talking on your phone? Shouldn't you be working on your project?"

Jax quickly called back, "I am. I'm working on my laptop...on...an...interactive program." He thought to himself, I don't want to worry my mom until I know more. And I really *am* on my laptop. And I really *am* interacting…with someone…or something.

"Make sure you're staying on track!" his mom called back.

"That was my mom," Jax explained. "I'm kind of in trouble because I didn't get a project for school done before our break."

"That's actually why I'm here!" Zaria exclaimed. "I have to do a project to pass the next step of my Zorketh training. On my planet, Zorketh is kind of like your school, but we study a lot about space because we can travel between the stars. Anyway, I have to find out three things about planet Earth and write a report to present to my classmates. I thought it would be fun to talk to an Earthling to do my research. Since Zix and Earth are in the same galaxy, I started to randomly monitor Earth frequencies. I happened on your conversation with your family and I decided to try to contact you. Traveling through space to get to your laptop was a snap."

The coincidence was almost too much. Almost.

Jax explained that his project was to find out three things about space and then write a report for *his* class.

It hit Zaria and Jax at the same time: they could help each other. This added a whole new meaning to working in groups! The only thing was, Jax wasn't sure how much he'd be able to say to his teacher and his class about Zaria and her expert help. They'd never believe him. *He* almost didn't believe it. Well, he wasn't going to worry about that now. Now was the time to decide on some topics they could work on together. Besides, Jax really wanted to keep this conversation going. After all, when else would he have a chance to talk with an alien about space?

Suddenly, the project and the school break were looking brighter. With the stars swirling around the room, it actually was a whole lot brighter.

"What do you know a lot about? On Earth, I mean," Zaria asked.

Jax thought—hard—and then said, "Well, we just learned about volcanoes. And hurricanes."

"Oh!" he added, gaining momentum. "I was just reading about auroras. How about auroras?"

"That's great!" Zaria said enthusiastically. "That would give me three things: volcanoes, hurricanes, and auroras."

"Your turn," Jax said. "What do you think I should do?"

"Well, how about black holes? Those are super interesting," Zaria said. "And supernovas…and stellar nurseries…and…."

"Wait!" It was Jax's turn to hold his hand up like he wanted to stop traffic. "That's three for me: black holes, supernovas, and stellar nurseries. Great!"

Zaria looked thoughtful. "You know, we have auroras on Zix. And we've had hurricanes, too. I think they aren't as extreme as the ones you have on Earth though, so my Zorketh teacher would want me to learn more about the ones you have. It's kind of neat, isn't it? We may be more alike than different."

"Well, where should we start?" Jax asked. "Maybe we can go back and forth. We can each do one topic and switch between Earth and space."

"Great idea!" Zaria said, which made Jax smile. "Let's start with black holes. I think you're going to be surprised when you find out what they're really like."

"I already know something about them," Jax protested.

"OK," Zaria said. "Tell me what you know about black holes and I'll go from there."

Jax said, "They're like giant vacuum cleaners. If you get near one, you get sucked in and you're never seen again. But sometimes, you can come out the other end into an alternate Universe."

"Is that what you think, Jax?" Zaria said dryly.

"Maybe I've been watching too many movies…." Jax replied quietly.

Jax's feelings were a bit hurt. He'd been hoping to impress Zaria with what he knew. Maybe she was wrong, he thought. Maybe black holes *were* like giant vacuum cleaners that were portals to other worlds. But deep down, he was sure that Zaria knew a lot more about things in space than he did. She had probably even been near a black hole. After all, she was from another world, and she'd know whether she'd travelled to Earth through a portal. Or not.

"Right. Now, watch this," Zaria said. "I'm going to show you a *black hole*."

And then the room started to change again.

Chapter 4 – Black Holes and Vacuum Cleaners

The stars started to whirl, faster and faster, until they were swirling around the center of the ceiling in Jax's room. It reminded Jax of water going down the drain in the bathroom, but upside down on his ceiling. Suddenly, other stars and planets and things that looked like big rocks were zooming across the ceiling.

But nothing was going down the drain! It just looked like nothing was in the center of the ceiling. It wasn't a big nothing. It was more like a dark patch the size of Jax's soccer ball.

Without warning, one of the very large stars near the nothingness seemed to extend a finger of material toward the nothingness. The star spun closer and closer toward the nothingness. When it got to the edge of the nothingness, Jax couldn't believe his eyes. Huge bright jets of what looked like gas from the star bounced against the edge of the nothingness and reached out to the far corners of the ceiling. Then, what was left of the star started to rotate into a disk. It fell into the nothingness and disappeared.

It was completely gone. Jax couldn't see anything left from the star. No light. No explosion. No jets of gas. No swirling disk.

Jax could feel his heart pounding. He looked around to see where Zaria was. She was still on his laptop screen, smiling at him.

"Well?" she said. "What do you think?"

"Wh-what WAS that?!" Jax could barely get the words out.

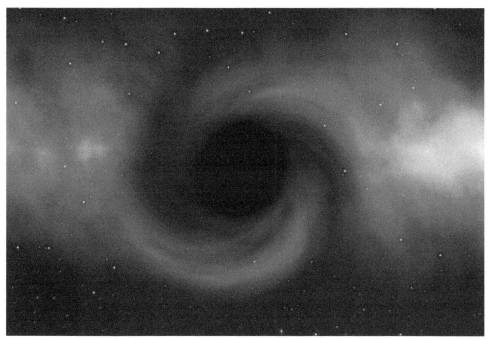

Black hole illustration

"That was a black hole," Zaria explained. "Would you like to know more?"

"Definitely!" Jax exclaimed. This was turning out way better than any project he'd ever done.

"OK," Zaria said. "Many black holes are formed from dying stars. Not all dying stars become black holes. And not all black holes are from dying stars. But what you just saw was a star that died and was eaten by a black hole. When that happens, the star's matter—the stuff it is made of—gets squeezed into a very, very tiny space. Then, the *gravity* of the black hole—its force of attraction—becomes so strong that even light can't get out."

"That's why I couldn't see anything at the end?" Jax said.

"That's right." Zaria could tell that Jax was getting it.

"But if we can't see black holes, how do we know they really exist?" Jax asked.

"Great question." said Zaria. "Earthlings now know for certain because experts used a collection of telescopes from around the Earth to obtain an image of the shadow of a black hole. It's at the center of M87, a galaxy that is a neighbor of our own Milky Way. They also use telescopes and satellites that are out in space to observe what happens to stars and things that get near to black holes."

"Like the star that was eaten?" Jax asked. He was amazed that he was so calm. After all, he was talking to an alien about a star that had just disappeared into a black hole in his bedroom!

"You've got it!" Zaria replied.

Jax realized that he had lots of questions to ask. "How big are black holes?"

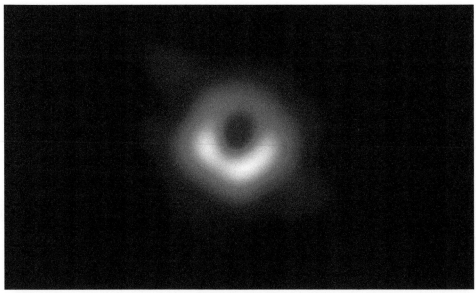

Black hole in M87

Zaria said, "Actually, there are three main categories of black holes. The smallest are called *primordial*. They may or may not actually exist. If they do, they are believed to be the size of just one *atom*, but with a lot of *mass*."

"I know that an atom is a tiny particle that is like a building block for matter, but what's mass?" Jax asked.

"Hmmm...mass is...stuff," Zaria answered. "Wait, that isn't a very good answer. Mass is the amount of matter that is in an object."

"One atom can't have a lot of stuff...I mean, mass," Jax said.

"Well, the mass that creates a black hole has been squeezed down. So in the smallest category of black hole, the primordial black hole, the mass is about the same as the mass in a large mountain."

"Wait a second." Jax added. "My best friend, Jefferson, has a trampoline in his backyard." Jax paused, thinking he'd better explain what a trampoline is. "A trampoline is a thing made of springy material that is stretched over a frame. It's fun to jump on it, but sometimes we like to just sit on it and talk. Once, Jefferson's Dad joined us. When he sat down, we all sunk so far into the trampoline, we had a hard time getting back up. Is that because Jefferson's Dad has more mass than we do?"

"Exactly." Zaria replied.

"That's awesome." Jax hoped that dinner wasn't going to be ready too soon. Even though he was hungry, he didn't want to stop talking with Zaria. "What are the other two main categories of black holes?"

Zaria was very happy that Jax was so interested in what she was telling him. "*Stellar black holes* are the most common. They can be formed by supernovas—exploded stars. They are much larger than primordial black holes. Stellar black holes are more than 10 times the mass of your Sun. You may not realize this, Jax, but there are lots of stellar black holes in our galaxy, the Milky Way."

Stellar black hole illustration

"No way." Jax could hardly believe it. "How many?"

"Experts aren't really sure, but the best estimate is that there are somewhere between 10 million and a billon." Zaria answered.

Jax was stunned. And a bit scared. "But if there are so many black holes, shouldn't we be afraid that the Earth might fall into one?"

Zaria laughed. Then she saw that Jax looked very anxious.

"Sorry for laughing, Jax." she apologized. "But no, the Earth will not fall into a black hole."

"How do you know?" Jax needed some reassurance.

"Because black holes don't go around gobbling up planets or stars or moons. Black holes like to stay in their own orbits, just like other objects in space tend to do. Earth is not orbiting a black hole, so you don't need to worry."

Zaria thought for a moment, and then added, "But pretend that for some impossible reason, a black hole replaced your Sun—which it never could. It would have the same mass as your Sun, which is not very much as black holes go. So, the planets would continue in their orbits instead of falling into it, because the pull of the black hole would not be strong enough to disturb the orbits of the planets—not even the closest planet to the Sun, Mercury. For a black hole as small as your Sun, a planet or other object would have to be about 2 miles—or 3 kilometers—away to fall in. Your Sun would need to be about 15 or 20 times even more massive than it is to become a black hole."

"We learned that the Sun won't burn out for billions of years anyway," Jax said, feeling better about all those black holes in the Milky Way. Then he asked, "What is the nearest black hole to Earth?"

Illustration of a supermassive black hole

"That's V616 Monocerotis," Zaria said. "It's about 6,000 light years away."

"I've heard of light years," Jax said, "But I don't know exactly what that means."

Can you think of a reason why we don't want our Sun to burn out?

"A *light year* is kind of what it sounds like. It's how far light can travel in a year. Light travels at about 186,000 miles per second, or about 300,000 kilometers per second," Zaria said. "That would be over 670,000,000 miles per hour," she added.

"Whoaaa!" Jax thought it over. "When we visit my grandparents, Mom drives 60 miles per hour on the highway. I thought that was fast, but light travels *really* fast!"

"And I had to travel even faster than that to get all the way to Earth from Zix." Zaria said. "But we can talk about that another time. Let's get back to black holes."

"OK," Jax said. "So far, we have primordial and stellar. What's the third main category?"

"Supermassive black holes," Zaria responded. "Experts think that every large galaxy has a *supermassive black hole* at its center. The mass of a supermassive black hole is more than a million of your Suns, and the biggest might even be as much as 40 billion

Suns. They might form from a very massive star collapsing into a black hole that then feeds on a lot of matter, but no one is sure."

"Is the Milky Way big enough to have a supermassive black hole?" Jax asked.

Spiral galaxy

"Yes! Earthlings call it *Sagittarius A-Star* but it's also known as Sagittarius A* or Sgr A*. Its mass is about 4 million Suns."

"Is the Earth near Sagittarius A*?" Jax was back to being a bit worried about black holes.

Zaria said, "Not at all! The Milky Way is a galaxy that looks like a spiral. The Earth is about two-thirds of the way from its center, in one of the arms of the spiral. Sagittarius A* is actually about 26,000 light years away from the Earth."

"Have you seen Sagittarius A*?" Jax asked.

"I've only seen the area around Sagittarius A*. It's actually between my planet and yours." Zaria said. "It's not very active for a black hole. Any stars it might attract are pretty far away from it. And remember, black holes don't go around searching for stars or planets to swallow."

Jax had an amusing thought. "Black holes are like The Three Bears! The Papa Bear is like a supermassive black hole. The Mama Bear is a stellar black hole. And the Baby Bear is a primordial black hole."

"I'm not familiar with that story. Maybe you can tell me about it sometime," Zaria said. "But I have a feeling that right now, it won't help with getting your report done, so let's keep going. What else can I tell you about black holes?"

Sagittarius A*

Jax thought for a few seconds and then asked, "What were those jets of gas that didn't go in the black hole?"

Zaria said, "Around the edge of a black hole is something called the *event horizon*. Any matter that crosses the event horizon falls into the black hole."

"And is neverrrr seen againnn!" Jax added in a dramatic voice.

"That's true," Zaria was quick to say, "But much matter never gets near an event horizon and what does get near can be blown away from it. Those jets of gas you saw were bouncing off before they crossed the event horizon of the black hole."

"So black holes really aren't giant vacuum cleaners sucking things in!" Jax exclaimed.

"You've got it!" Zaria looked as excited as Jax felt.

Then she said, "Black holes aren't all that bad. In fact, supermassive black holes may even help to hold galaxies together, and they help recycle matter through their galaxies. You can think of them like giant cosmic recycling centers because some of the material shooting out from around the black hole into the galaxy can help form new generations of stars and other stuff, like us, eventually."

"So, I am partly made of stuff from stars? That's so cool. What else can you tell me?" Jax was really curious and wanted to know everything that Zaria could tell him.

"*Spaghettification*," Zaria said.

"Spaghetti-fi-what?!" Jax suddenly remembered that he was hungry.

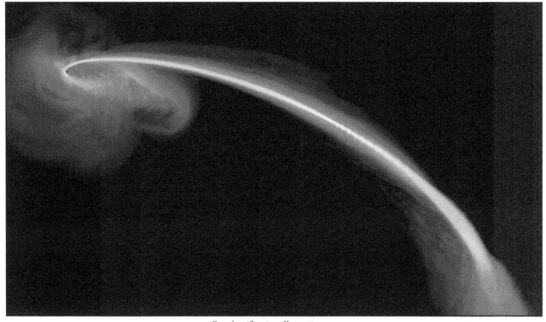

Spaghettification illustration

"Spaghettification. It's how the gravity of a black hole can pull apart a star that falls into it. The gravity of a black hole gets stronger the closer the star gets. It will pull with the most force on the part of the star closest to it. Whatever part of the star is closest to the black hole's gravity will get stretched out like a piece of spaghetti."

How can black holes be like water going down a drain?

Now Jax was hoping that his mom was making pasta for dinner. "So on Earth, when I'm standing up, the gravity is stronger at my feet than at my head?"

"Right." Zaria was thrilled with how quickly Jax understood what she told him.

Jax heard his mom calling, "Jackson, it's time for dinner!"

"I've got to go," Jax said to Zaria. "Will you be here when I get back after dinner?"

"I sure hope so" Zaria replied. "After all, it's your turn to help me."

Black Hole Activity

You will need:
1. A large square piece of material that is stretchy. A piece of spandex will work well. It should be at least 12" on each side, but up to 20" on each side is better.
2. A ball that is heavy. For a smaller square of material, use a golf ball. For larger squares of material, you can use baseball, croquet ball, or cricket ball.
3. A ball that is light. A marble works well, or a small ball bearing.

What to do:
1. Ask two or more people to stretch the square of material and hold it still.
2. Roll the heavier ball onto the material. Let it stop in the middle of the square. Notice that it will make an indentation.
3. Roll the lighter ball onto the material. It will rotate until it stops up against the heavier ball.
4. Now, make a hole in the center of the material, large enough for the smaller ball to fit through.
5. Roll balls onto the material again, this time, rolling the smaller ball first.

Observe:
1. The first time you roll the balls, the heavier ball will look like it is attracting the lighter ball, much like how a black hole's gravity attracts objects that get too close to it.
2. Once the lighter ball stops next to the heavier ball, it cannot "escape." This is how the gravity of a black hole prevents anything that gets too close to it from leaving.
3. The second time you roll the balls onto the material, the smaller ball will fall through the hole, "disappearing" into the "black hole." The larger ball will not fall through. It will continue to rotate around the center of the material.

Chapter 5 – Volcanoes and "Zatcheries"

Jax sat at his usual place at the kitchen table. He was practically drooling when he saw his mom with a platter of spaghetti and meatballs—his favorite dinner. Gwen came dashing to her place with both thumbs flying on her phone as she texted Ellie.

"Gwen, you know the rules. No phones at the table." Clara said.

Gwen put her phone down and when she thought Clara wasn't looking, she stuck her tongue out at Jax.

"FFFFF," Jax said in Gwen's direction.

"Mommmmm. He's doing it again!" Gwen complained.

Clara sometimes felt like she needed to get a referee's whistle. "OK, you two. Enough. Let's enjoy a nice, calm dinner. Gwen, what do you have planned for this weekend?"

"I was just texting with Ellie. She invited me to sleep over at her house tonight. Her dad can pick me up right after dinner. And you can get me tomorrow after Jax's soccer practice."

"But Mom, it's Gwen's turn to do the dishes, and I want to get back to working on my project!" complained Jax.

"Just because you and President Jefferson are behind on your schoolwork doesn't mean I have to suffer," Gwen retorted. "Besides, I walked Ollie for you yesterday after school when you had soccer practice."

Clara felt even more like a referee than before. "Let's stop keeping score and help each other out. Jax, please lend a hand with the dishes so Gwen can have her sleepover with Ellie."

Jax realized that it was probably a good idea for Gwen to be out of the house tonight. That way, he wouldn't be worried that she might barge into his room and find Zaria there.

"Sure, that's fine." Jax said.

The rest of dinner was uneventful. As Jax cleared the table, his mom asked, "So, how is the project coming along?"

Jax smiled and said, "Great! Did you know that black holes aren't really giant cosmic vacuum cleaners? They don't go through the Universe gobbling everything up like Pac Man. And if something gets too close to one, it can be stretched out like a piece of the spaghetti we just ate."

Clara was impressed. "That's amazing, Jax. I'd really like to read all about it when you're done. It sounds like I'd learn a lot."

Jax felt happy. "Sure, Mom. I'm going to get back to it now. I'm about to dive into volcanoes. Not really...you know what I mean."

"Volcanoes?" Clara asked. "I thought your project was about space."

Jax thought quickly and said. "Yes, but there are volcanoes in space, too."

"Ok, cool, off you go. And don't forget to take Ollie out in a bit."

"I won't forget." Jax said. "C'mon, boy."

Ollie followed Jax to his room, wagging his tail in the hope of an after-dinner treat, and looking like he was wondering if he'd get to talk to that girl again, too.

Jax was happy to see Zaria waiting for him on his laptop screen. He was half afraid that he'd dreamed the whole thing.

"Hi!" Zaria said. "I'm ready to hear about volcanoes."

"I can't really turn my room into a volcano the way you did with the black hole," Jax said. "Wait! Maybe I can."

Jax went to his closet, reached far in the back of the shelf, and pulled out his science fair project from last year. It was a model of a volcano, set up on a metal tray. He still had the packet of the ingredients to make it look like it was erupting.

"Watch this!" Jax exclaimed. He quickly mixed the leftover vinegar, dish detergent, and baking soda, and poured it into the volcano.

The volcano erupted, and Zaria laughed and clapped her hands. "Way cool!"

"Did you know," Jax asked, "That on my planet, the word *volcano* comes from the name of the ancient Roman god of fire, Vulcan? That really fits, because volcanoes are openings in the Earth that can erupt with a lot of force and heat. But they don't always do that."

Kilauea volcano erupting

"And they aren't just on Earth," Zaria added. "I think I flew by volcanoes on Mars on my way here."

"Exactly." Jax said. "Other planets and even moons can have volcanoes. And they can be underwater, too."

"But what is the stuff that comes out of a volcano?" Zaria asked.

"There's different stuff," Jax said. "Let's see…there's magma, and lava, and gas."

"I know what gas is," Zaria replied. "But what are magma and lava?"

"Well, the hot liquid that is inside a volcano is called *magma*. Once it leaves the volcano, it's called *lava*. Lava is super-hot. It can be over 2,200 degrees Fahrenheit." Jax answered.

Jax wasn't sure if Zaria understood the metric system better, so he added, "That's over 1,200 degrees Celsius."

"That would burn everything in its path." Zaria noted.

"That's true. And lava can be thin and runny, or it can be so thick that it clogs the opening of the volcano. When that happens, pressure can build up inside the volcano and cause an eruption."

Zaria asked, "Does lava act the same way underwater?"

"It's still lava, but when it's underwater it's called *pillow lava* because it forms shapes that look like pillows," Jax said, pointing to the pillow on his bed.

All of the things that Jax had learned from doing his science fair project were rushing back into his head. "There's another thing that happens when a volcano erupts. It can throw ash high into the air. I mean, really high, as high as 17 miles—that's 30 kilometers—above the Earth! And the ash can be dangerous."

Volcano erupting in Clark National Park, Alaska

"Why would it be dangerous?" Zaria was really curious about that.

"Well," Jax said, "The ash is made of bits of burnt rock that form a kind of dust called an *ash cloud*. The ash cloud can reach the atmosphere and spread around the Earth. It can be harmful to breathe. If it's really thick, it's not safe for planes to fly through it."

"Whoaaa!" Zaria paused and then wanted to know, "Has that ever happened?"

"Yes!" Jax picked up the globe behind his laptop and moved it so Zaria could see where he pointed. "When I was only a baby, a volcano in Iceland erupted and airports all over Europe had to be closed. My dad was in England when it happened. He couldn't get home for almost a week."

"That must have been tough." Zaria said.

"Yes," Jax told her. "My mom said that he didn't have enough clean clothes. And even worse, he wasn't home in time for my sister's birthday. Do you celebrate birthdays on Zix?"

How might being in an ash cloud be similar to being in smoke from a fire?

"If you mean the day that you came into being, yes," Zaria said. "Only we call them 'zatcheries' because Zixians are hatched."

"Wow, really?" Jax asked. "I hope you get presents and cake, too."

"It's kind of the other way around. We celebrate by giving our family and friends special treats. It's really fun. Anyway, let's get back to volcanoes. What other kinds of volcanoes do you have on Earth?" Zaria asked.

Jax continued, "Some volcanoes have big craters on top of them, called *calderas*. There are two ways that calderas can form. One is when a volcano erupts and collapses in on itself. The other way is when a volcano erupts so violently it blasts its top off."

"So…if I wanted to see a volcano on Earth, where could I go?" Zaria asked.

"Good question!" Jax smiled. He was pleased that Zaria was as interested in volcanoes as he was about black holes. He picked up the globe again. "There are over 80 volcanoes on the ocean floors, mostly in the Pacific Ocean, there," Jax pointed. "But you'd need a special submarine to see those. Volcanoes can be under ice caps, too, like the one that erupted in Iceland. Some are also deep inside the *mantle* of the Earth. That's the Earth's middle layer."

"There must be *some* volcanoes that are easier to see!" Zaria exclaimed.

"I'm getting to those!" Jax responded. "About 90% of the volcanoes on Earth are in what is called *The Ring of Fire*. That's an area around the Pacific Ocean that is shaped like a horseshoe. It covers over 25,000 miles, or 40,000 kilometers."

"Why are so many volcanoes there?" Zaria wanted to know.

"Well…" Jax thought about how to explain what he wanted to say. "It has to do with the movement of *tectonic plates*."

"Is that 'plate' as in something humans eat food on?" Zaria was full of questions.

"Ummm…not really. Unless you had a huge appetite!" Jax answered. "Tectonic plates are gigantic portions of the *Earth's crust*. That's the top layer of the Earth. They kind of fit together like giant pieces of a puzzle. But there are *fault lines* at the boundaries of tectonic plates. Fault lines are cracks in the Earth's crust. Where there are fault lines, the tectonic plates can move. Sometimes they slide one on top of another, or they slide apart, or they slide up or down alongside each other. When they do, volcanoes—and earthquakes—can occur.

How are the layers of the Earth like a layer cake?

"So, why don't people just move away from the fault lines?" Zaria wondered.

Jax replied, "That would be hard to do, because there are faults all over the Earth, not just at the boundaries of tectonic plates. In school we learned that about one out of every 20 people on Earth live within the range of a volcano."

"Sounds dangerous." Zaria said. "I think I'll stay on Zix!"

"Zix probably has dangers, too, and I'd like to hear about them. But right now, there's still more to tell you about volcanoes for your project."

Before he could continue, Jax's phone beeped with the ringtone assigned to Jefferson. "Hold on a sec, Zaria. My best friend, Jefferson, wants to know what time to pick me up for soccer practice tomorrow."

"You're going to *sock a girl*?!" Zaria was stunned.

"Not sock her, soccer!" Jax laughed. "It's a sport. If you like, I'll tell you about that another time, too. Right now, I just need to send Jeff a quick text."

When he was done, Jax said, "OK. Here's something you'll want to know. Just like with black holes, there are three main categories of volcanoes."

"Like your three bears again?" Zaria asked.

"Not exactly." Jax said. "Volcanoes are active, dormant, or extinct. *Active volcanoes* are likely to explode again."

"Are there lots of those on Earth?" Zaria wanted to know.

"There are almost 2,000 active volcanoes. At any time, there are usually about 20 volcanoes that are erupting somewhere on Earth." Jax told her.

"Even now?" Zaria seemed surprised.

"Yes!" Jax said. "But they aren't all super explosive with stuff flying up into the air. Some have lava that flows gently out of their *vents*. A vent is the opening in a volcano."

Dormant volcano in Indonesia

Jax continued. "The other two categories are *dormant volcanoes* and *extinct volcanoes*. Dormant volcanoes are volcanoes that erupted in the past but aren't expected to erupt again soon. And extinct volcanoes are volcanoes that haven't erupted in a long time and aren't likely to erupt ever again."

Jax thought for a second. "So, maybe volcanoes *are* like bears! A dormant volcano is like a bear that's hibernating—sleeping through the winter. When it wakes up, it's hungry and you don't want to get in its way. That would make the bear more like an active volcano."

"What about the extinct part?" Zaria asked. "Is that if the bear didn't wake up...ever?"

"Ummm...I guess." Jax didn't like thinking about that. "Let's not go there!"

Zaria agreed. "Good idea."

"How about if we talk about the shapes of volcanoes?" Jax suggested.

"OK!" Zaria was glad that Jax knew so much to tell her. All of this information was sure to help her write a good report for the next part of her Zorketh training.

Jax said, "Not all volcanoes look like mountains. The ones that look like mountains or cones are called *composite volcanoes*. They get formed from layers of lava that have built up over many years. Some are huge. They can be over 8,000 feet tall. That's over 2,400 meters."

"Whoaaa!" Zaria exclaimed.

Molten lava

"You've got that right!" Jax agreed. "C*inder cone volcanoes* look like cones, too. They just aren't as tall as composite volcanoes. They only get to be about 1,000 feet, or 300 meters." Jax went on, "But other volcanoes are flat or kind of shaped like a bowl. Those are called *shield volcanoes*. But I think that *lava domes* are the most interesting volcanoes of all. They form when lava is so thick, it can't flow. It builds up around the volcano's vent until there is so much pressure, it erupts. Sometimes, lava domes even form inside other types of volcanoes."

The next time the top of your toothpaste gets crusty and you have to push it out, think of a lava dome

"Very cool…I mean, hot!" Zaria laughed and Jax joined in.

"Earth would look very different without volcanoes." Jax said. "They've played an important part in forming mountains and islands."

"So islands can be volcanoes that are partly underwater?" Zaria was fascinated.

"Uh-huh." Jax nodded his head. "The islands that form Hawaii in the Pacific Ocean are a good example of that."

"Are they in the Ring of Fire?" Zaria asked.

Jax said, "Yes. The Earth's largest active volcano is on the Big Island in Hawaii. It's called Mauna Loa. The tallest volcano on Earth is there, too. It is right next to Mauna Loa. Its name is Mauna Kea. They are shield volcanoes. You only see part of them. They go way below the ocean floor deep into the Earth's crust."

"Volcanoes really have changed the way the Earth looks!" Zaria exclaimed. "Zix doesn't have volcanoes but I know that other planets do."

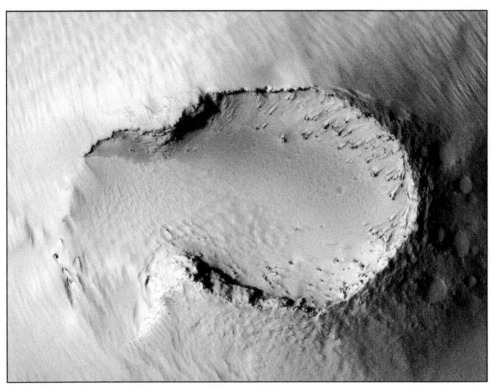

Volcano on Mars

"Yes, you noticed the volcanoes on Mars," Jax said. "Well, the tallest volcano that we know about in our solar system is on Mars. It's a shield volcano called Olympus Mons. It is almost three times as tall as the tallest mountain on Earth, Mt. Everest."

"But it's extinct, right?" Zaria asked.

"Or maybe dormant," Jax replied. "There's a new space mission planned to go to Mars. I hope we find out then."

Zaria smiled. "Maybe your technology will let you come visit me on Zix one day!"

Jax liked the thought of that.

Did you know? Mauna means mountain in Hawaiian.

"Another nearby planet, Venus, has volcanoes but its atmosphere is very thick so they're hard to see." Jax said. "And the moons of Jupiter, Saturn, and Neptune all have active volcanoes."

Zaria said, "We learned about those in our Zorketh training. It was something about a discovery by your NASA's Voyager 1 spacecraft."

Volcano on Venus

"That's right, Voyager has been exploring my solar system since well before I was born." Jax added, "Voyager sent the first images we ever saw of an erupting volcano outside of Earth. It was on Jupiter's moon, Io. In fact, Io has the most active volcano that we know of in the solar system. It's so active that it changes the surface of Io all the time!"

"Any other interesting volcanoes?" Zaria asked.

"Lots!" Jax replied.

"How about if you tell me your three favorites," Zaria suggested.

"Hmmm…let's see. I think third place would be Mount St. Helen's in Washington State in the United States," Jax said. "The last time it erupted was in 2008. I like that one because it was a lava dome volcano that shifted to let its hot gases escape."

He thought again, "My second favorite volcano happened back in 1883 in Southeast Asia. That was Mount Krakatoa. When it erupted, it released so much energy that it made one of the loudest sounds ever recorded in Earth's history."

Zaria thought it would be hard for Jax to top either of those. "What is your favorite?"

Mount St. Helens

"Easy!" Jax smiled. "My favorite of all time is Mount Vesuvius in Italy. It's an active volcano. In the year 79AD, it erupted and completely destroyed the city of Pompeii. Its ash preserved the whole city and the people who were caught in it. I hope I can visit there someday."

"Volcanoes can be pretty nasty," Zaria observed.

"Yes, but they have some interesting uses, too." Jax reassured her.

"Really?" Zaria was eager to hear what was good about volcanoes.

"Some people choose to live on the sides of volcanoes, because the soil is fertile. They grow their crops there. And there is a bird in Indonesia—that's a country made up of islands between Asia and Australia—called a maleo bird. It buries its eggs in the soil or sand by a volcano to keep them warm. After the chicks hatch, they use their claws to climb out to the surface."

"That's so clever." Zaria said. "Anything else?"

"One more thing." Jax added. "There's a volcanic rock that is called *pumice*. It's so light and airy that it can float. But it's rough and scratchy, too. My mom has some to smooth her dry skin."

"I think I have enough on volcanoes for my report for my Zorketh training, Jax. Thanks!" Zaria said. "Are you ready to return to space?"

"Am I ever!" Jax exclaimed. "Supernovas, here I come!"

Volcano Activity

You can make your own volcano, like the one Jax showed Zaria.

You will need:
1. A tray with sides
2. Paper towels on the tray, especially if you're doing this inside!
3. An empty jar, plastic cup, or plastic soft drink bottle
4. Enough water to fill the jar, cup, or bottle 2/3 full
5. Some clay in a color that looks like it would be a volcano
6. A bowl
7. 1 cup of vinegar
8. 1 teaspoon of dish detergent
9. A few drops of food coloring
10. A funnel
11. A paper towel or some tissue
12. 4 tablespoons of baking soda
13. An elastic band or some string

What to do:
1. Line the tray with paper towels to absorb any mess from the eruption.
2. Put the water in the jar, cup, or bottle.
3. Build your volcano on the tray, using the clay around the jar, cup, or bottle.
4. Let the clay dry.
5. Mix the vinegar, detergent, and food coloring in the bowl.
6. Use the funnel to pour the mixture into the jar, cup, or bottle.
7. Wrap the baking soda in a paper towel or tissue and loosely tie it with the string or an elastic band.
8. Add the baking soda packet to the volcano's vent.

Observe:
1. The baking powder will react with the other ingredients and cause your volcano to erupt!

Chapter 6 – I Have a Bit of a Supernova in Me

Ollie had other ideas. He started woofing softly toward Zaria. Jax knew he was talking to her.

"What's up with Ollie?" Jax asked.

"Ollie wants me to remind you that he needs to go for a walk," Zaria replied. "Why does he need to go for a walk right now?"

"Ummm…" Jax hesitated, blushing a bit. "He needs to…go…do his business." Jax was trying to be as delicate as possible.

"Your dog is in business? And it involves walking somewhere?" Zaria looked very confused.

"Noooo…" Jax tried again. He realized that he'd have to come right out and say it. "Ollie needs to relieve himself. Go to the bathroom. Pee. And Poo. Dogs do that outside, and humans scoop it into a bag to dispose it." Then Jax added, "The poo. Not the pee."

Zaria looked at Ollie and asked him, "Really? Or is Jax teasing me?" Ollie woofed a reply to her.

"OK, Jax," Zaria said. "Seems odd to me, but Ollie not only said that's true, he said to tell you that he needs to go out *right now!*"

"C'mon, Ollie," Jax said. Then he said to Zaria, "We won't be long."

"That's what Ollie said, too." she commented.

When they returned, Ollie woofed a greeting to Zaria.

"Ollie wants a treat for being a good boy," Zaria told Jax.

"Yeesh, Ollie. I'm not so sure I like it that you can talk to Zaria." But Jax really didn't mind. And he always gave Ollie a treat when they came in after a walk anyway.

Jax gave Ollie his treat and then said, "Supernovas, here I come!"

"I'm not certain you want to be in the middle of a supernova, Jax." Zaria cautioned. "They're all about explosions."

Jax smiled, "Great! The bigger, the better!"

"OK, you asked for it!" Zaria said. "As you humans say, 'Buckle your seatbelt.' This one might throw you off your chair!"

Jax held tightly onto the arms of his desk chair. Then, his room went dark again.

A large star came into view near his ceiling. He could hear a humming sound as the star appeared to collapse in on itself. Will this fall into another black hole, Jax wondered? But before it could do that, the star exploded in the brightest, most magnificent display of light and force that Jax had ever seen. Spectacular jets of material flew out from the star in opposite directions, travelling faster than Jax could track them.

Jax spoke quietly, "Whoaaa! I thought the fireworks on the Fourth of July were special. This is *unreal*!"

"But it *is* real. Sort of. I mean, as real as it can be," Zaria said. Then she asked, "Now that you've seen a supernova, would you like to know about them?"

"You bet!" Jax answered. He was in awe of what he had just seen.

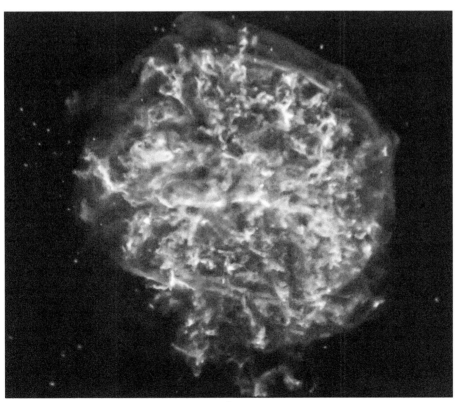

Supernova

"OK," Zaria said. "A *supernova* is a star that explodes. In fact, supernovas are some of the largest explosions that happen in the Universe. A star can become a supernova if it's at the end of its life. And remember when we talked about mass? Well, a star needs a certain amount of mass to explode as a supernova. Too much or too little, and it won't become a supernova."

"It's like the porridge in the three bears story!" Jax exclaimed. "A supernova's mass needs to be just right."

"I'm definitely going to have to read that story, Jax," Zaria remarked.

"I know that our Sun doesn't have enough mass to become a black hole. And it can't explode as a supernova someday, right?" Jax asked.

"Right! Your Sun doesn't have enough mass to explode as a supernova, either. There are other stars in our galaxy that might, though. I'll tell you about those in a bit," Zaria said. "First, I want to tell you a few other things about supernovas."

Jax interrupted with a question. "Wait! First, tell me what that humming sound was."

"Good place to start, Jax!" Zaria exclaimed. "Just before they explode, stars that are about to become supernovas vibrate. That vibration is what you heard."

"It's like when my sister plays her music too loud," Jax observed. "My mom always tells her to turn it down because the speakers start to vibrate and make a funny humming sound."

"That's right." Zaria smiled.

"Well, it doesn't help that my mom doesn't exactly like Gwen's music." Jax smiled back. "That's probably the real reason she tells my sister to turn it down."

"My parents don't like my music, either. I guess some things are the same all over the Universe," Zaria sighed.

Jax said, "You said that a supernova is one of the largest explosions that happens in the Universe. How big is it?"

"A supernova explosion is so big that for a short time, it can shine brighter than an entire galaxy," Zaria explained. "Then it will start to fade, but that can take weeks or even months. Actually, it's possible for one supernova to radiate more energy than your Sun will over its entire existence."

"No wonder it was so bright. It looked like those jets coming out of it were going really fast, too." Jax observed.

"They sure were!" Zaria said. "The stuff that comes out of a supernova can travel as fast as 40,000 kilometers per second. That's 25,000 miles. That means that one of those jets could go completely around the equator of the Earth in just one second."

"I could be home again almost before I left!" Jax exclaimed.

"For sure! No one would even know you'd been gone." Zaria laughed.

"Cool." Jax said, thinking of the possibilities of travelling that fast. Then he asked, "If a supernova is different from a black hole, what happens to the middle of the star? And what happens to those jets?"

Zaria answered, "Well, the core of the star can become a *neutron star*. That's the smallest and most dense star that we know of. The leftover material continues to expand out into the Universe. That's what is called a *supernova remnant*. And billions and billions of atoms that are flung out form colorful *nebulas*. Those are clouds of dust and gases. If you have a small telescope, you can see a supernova remnant in your own night sky. It's called the Crab Nebula. It's from a supernova that exploded almost 1,000 of your years ago."

Crab Nebula

"I read that supernovas can form new stars, too. Is that right?" Jax wanted to know.

"Yes!" Zaria replied. "That's one of the really important things about supernovas. The material they spread can become compressed and form new generations of stars. Something else I think you'll like to know is that much of everything on Earth—including you and Ollie – is made of elements that came from star material."

"Hey Ollie, how great is it that we have parts of stars in us?!" Jax exclaimed. Ollie woofed and wagged his tail in delight.

Zaria smiled. "You sure do! And so do I. Elements like carbon, iron, and nitrogen are just a few of the ones that came from supernovas. The calcium in your bones and the oxygen you breathe also came from supernovas. So did the silicon in your laptop."

"It's like we were brewed up somewhere far away. I really like that!" Jax said. Then he asked, "How often do stars explode as supernovas?"

"I'm not certain that we know," Zaria said. "I've read that there is one supernova explosion every second somewhere in Universe. It could be more, though. Some estimates are as many as 10 per second."

"How about in our galaxy, in the Milky Way?" Jax wondered.

"The average in our galaxy is about one supernova explosion happening every 50 Earth years," Zaria said. "Oh, I almost forgot to tell you! There are two main types of supernovas."

How is the number of supernovas exploding in the Universe like popcorn exploding in a microwave oven?

"Only two? There goes the three bears idea." Jax teased.

"Well, the first is called a *Type I supernova*, or more correctly, a *Type 1a*," Zaria began. "A Type I supernova needs two stars in what is known as a *binary star system*."

"We learned in school that 'binary' means two," Jax said.

"Yes, and for a Type I supernova, one of those stars is called a *white dwarf*. A white dwarf is a star that is close to the end of its life. It has used up most of its fuel and is in the process of collapsing," Zaria said. "The other star is called a *companion star*."

"Do they crash into each other?" Jax guessed.

"Not quite. What happens is that the white dwarf star uses its gravitational pull to take matter from the companion star."

"That's stealing!" Jax exclaimed. "White dwarf stars are thieves!"

"Not a bad way to think of it," Zaria said. "The thing is, at some point the white dwarf star takes too much matter from the companion star. Just like a thief who doesn't get caught at first and keeps stealing, it eventually gets into trouble. In the white dwarf's case, it explodes into a supernova."

Jax thought for a second, "But I only saw one star when you showed me a supernova."

"And that's a *Type II supernova*," Zaria said. "I think they're much more exciting to see."

"So, what happens to cause a Type II supernova?" Jax asked.

"A Type II supernova is a star that is running out of its fuel," Zaria explained. "But it doesn't have a companion star. Instead, it starts to collapse under its own gravity. As it does, the heavier elements in it build up in its center and the lighter elements get layered on its outside."

"What happens then?" Jax asked.

"Well, the star can eventually become a *red supergiant*. When the core gets too heavy, it can't handle its own gravitational pull. It starts to fall in on itself. Eventually, the imploding reaches a certain point where the outer layers bounce back out, off of the star's core. That's when the explosion happens."

"Hold on!" Jax said. "There are three types of stars in supernova explosions? White dwarfs, companion stars, and red supergiants?"

Zaria held up her hand to stop him. "Is this the three bears thing again, Jax?"

"Ummm…maybe…." Jax replied.

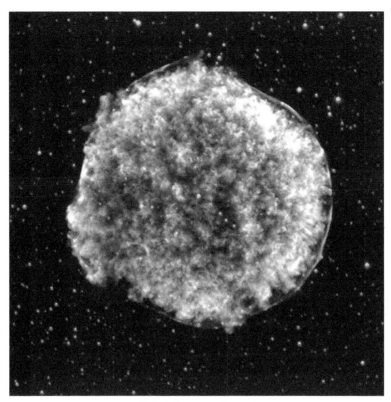

Tycho's Supernova Remnant

How is a Type II supernova like an onion?

"What is it with you and that story?!" Zaria laughed. "How about we leave the three bears and just talk about supernovas in our galaxy?"

"Sure." Jax said, but he promised himself that he'd read The Three Bears to Zaria at some point.

"My favorite supernova remnant in the Milky Way is one that Earthlings call Cassiopeia A, or CasA for short. It's about 10,000 light years from Earth. I like it because it's really beautiful and because it's moving outward at a really fast speed. It could travel from the Earth to the Earth's moon in 30 seconds!"

"That's pretty fast," Jax said.

"Uh-huh," Zaria said. "Another supernova was seen much more recently by people on your planet, only a few decades ago in 1987. It was in one of the galaxies that is close to ours, called the Large Magellanic Cloud. It's so close that it is being observed as it continues to change. It's really teaching us on Zix a lot about supernovas!"

"Are there any supernovas that might happen soon in the Milky Way?" Jax asked.

"No one can predict exactly when a star will go supernova," Zaria said. "But there is a red supergiant called Betelgeuse in the Milky Way. It's near the end of its life. You can see it if you look in your constellation Orion. It's the brightest star in that constellation. It could explode soon...or not for millions of years."

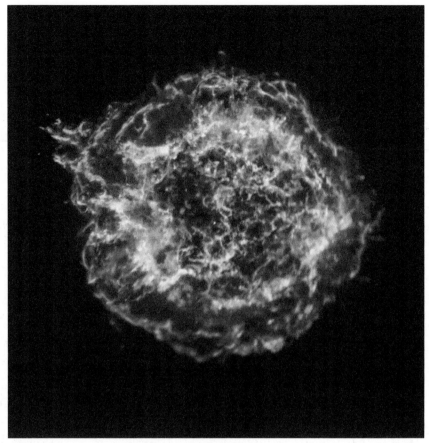

Cassiopeia A

"So…if it's only one star, it will be a Type II supernova, right?" Jax asked.

"Right!" Zaria replied. "But even if it happened tomorrow, you don't have to worry about being hurt by it."

Jax was relieved. "Why?"

"Because it's too far away. It's over 600 light years from the Earth. So, Earthlings will be able to see the explosion with no worries."

"Well, that's good." Jax said. "I wish I could see a real supernova as it happened."

"You might, Jax!" Zaria was very encouraging. "You don't have to be a scientist to discover important things in space, like supernovas. I learned that just a few years ago, a 14-year-old Earthling girl was looking through her telescope and discovered a supernova in the constellation Pegasus. In fact, you don't even need a telescope to make a discovery. A 10-year-old Earthling girl was looking at images on her computer and discovered a supernova in the constellation Camelopardalis. She's the youngest person on your planet ever to find a supernova!"

Hearing that, Jax felt more determined than ever to have a career where he could work on something to do with space. And now he had a friend from another planet. He was more certain than ever that he could really reach his goal.

Betelgeuse

"Hellooo…. Are you there, Jax? You look as if you are as far away as Betelgeuse. What are you thinking?" Zaria asked.

"Nothing much." Jax wasn't ready to share his future plans with Zaria. Not yet.

"Oh, I've lost track of the time!" Zaria realized. "I need to check in back on Zix or my parents will wonder what I'm up to."

"I understand all about that." Jax said. Then he added, "As long as you come back!"

"Of course I'll be back," Zaria said. "We still have a lot to do before we can finish our projects. I hope we can talk about auroras next."

"Great idea." Jax said. "Anyway, it's kind of late here. I need to get some sleep and then go to soccer practice in the morning. How about if we get back to work on our projects tomorrow after my lunchtime?"

"Works for me!" Zaria said. With a wave and a smile, she disappeared.

Jax was sure that Zaria would be back tomorrow. At least he was pretty sure. And he couldn't wait to talk to her again.

Supernova Activity

To get an idea of what supernova jets are like, try this activity:

You will need:
1. A large ball, like a soccer ball or a basketball
2. A small ball, like a tennis ball or a ping-pong ball

What to do:
1. Make sure you do this outside on a hard surface, like a paved driveway or sidewalk.
2. Bounce the larger ball and notice how high it bounces.
3. Bounce the smaller ball and notice how high it bounces.
4. Hold the smaller ball on top of the larger ball about 3 feet (a meter) off of the ground. This will be easier if someone helps to hold the balls.
5. Let go of the two balls at the same time.

Observe:
1. What happens to the balls? You will see that when the balls are dropped together, the larger ball does not bounce as high as it did the first time, and then it stops. That represents the core of the dying star collapsing in on itself.
2. The smaller ball is like the outside layers of the dying star. The downward momentum from the fall of the larger ball transfers up to the smaller ball. It will be thrust into the air much higher than it was originally, like the jets of a supernova!

Chapter 7 – Auroras and Losing Track of Time

"Hey Jaaaxxx…are you in there?" Jefferson asked.

"Oh, yeah." Jax brought his mind back to Earth and soccer practice. "I was just…thinking about our project."

"Now? During soccer practice? C'mon, Jax, it isn't like we don't need this practice," Jeff said. "We need to beat the Wildcats next week or we won't be in the playoffs!"

Jax did his best to concentrate, but he kept thinking about Zaria. He wondered what Jeff would say if he knew that a real live alien was helping him with his project. And that he was helping her, too. What was that thing she needed to pass? Oh, right, the next step of her Zorketh training. He didn't want to say anything to Jeff, though. Not yet, anyway.

After practice, Jeff said, "Hey, wanna hang after lunch? A bunch of us could go play baseball in the park."

"Nahhh…I can't," Jax replied. "I have to get back to my project. Fish Fart Face told my mom that I've known about the assignment for weeks."

"Are you grounded?" Jeff asked. He knew that Mrs. Bishop was really nice but she could be strict when it came to school stuff.

"No," Jax said, "But she kinda said that I'd better finish it so it isn't hanging over me all week."

"OK, but text me if you change your mind. We can ride our bikes together to the ball field," Jeff said. Then he remembered. "My family is going out for pizza tonight. Wanna come? Pizza's good brain food!"

Jax laughed, "On what planet is pizza good brain food, Jeff?!" But pizza did sound good. And he did have to eat. And then Gwen couldn't stick him with cleaning up after dinner again. He asked Jeff, "You sure it'll be OK with your parents?"

"Of course. We'll pick you up at 6," Jeff said.

"See you then," Jax said, and went to look for his mom's car in the parking area near the soccer field.

When he got home, Jax made a peanut butter and jelly sandwich for lunch. "Hey, Mom," he said. "Jeff invited me to go out with his family for pizza tonight. Is that OK?"

Clara said, "That's fine. There's just enough leftover spaghetti for two, so Gwen and I can have that."

Jax smiled. "Thanks. I'm going to work on my project until Jeff comes to pick me up. He said he'd be here at 6."

"I'm glad you're being so responsible, Jax. I'm sure you'd rather be out with your friends this afternoon," Clara said. "You'll have your project done in no time and then you can relax and have fun for the rest of the break."

It occurred to Jax that getting his project done quickly might not be such a good idea. He was enjoying his time with Zaria. If they finished their projects, she might go back to Zix and never return. He pushed that thought away. After all, maybe she'd have more Zorketh training to do and he could keep helping her. And she could teach him lots more about space.

Jax ran to his room with Ollie close by. He closed his door and opened his laptop. Nothing happened. "Zaria?" he called quietly.

Nothing.

"Zaria? Are you there?" he tried again. Still nothing.

Jax's heart sunk. The peanut butter and jelly sandwich felt like a rock in his stomach. Just as he was about to text Jeff that maybe he'd go to the park to play baseball after all, his laptop screen lit up.

"You're here!" Jax exclaimed.

Zaria answered, "Of course I'm here."

"I thought…maybe…you forgot…or something…." Jax didn't know quite what to say.

"Jax, I don't know about humans, but when beings from Zix say they're going to be someplace, they get there!" Zaria smiled. "I guess I lost track of time again, though. I was telling my parents what we're doing. They were really interested in hearing all about you."

"You told your parents about me? And that we're working together?" Jax was surprised.

"Of course! You didn't tell your mom?" Zaria asked.

Jax thought for a second. "Ummm, no. Well, not yet. It hasn't really come up." Jax thought that his mom might be OK about him making friends with an alien, but if she weren't, then what? But he knew he really would have to tell her soon.

Keeping secrets from your parents wasn't a cool idea.

"OK," Zaria said. "Well, back to our projects. It's your turn. I'm ready to hear all about the Earth's auroras."

"I'm glad you mentioned that you have auroras on Zix," Jax said, "because otherwise I'm not sure how I could create one to show you. I guess we could start by looking at some pictures of them."

Jax took down one of his favorite books from his bookcase, one he used to read with his Dad. He looked through it until he found the picture he wanted to show Zaria. "Here is one of my favorite pictures of an aurora. Isn't it awesome?"

Aurora Borealis seen from Sweden

Zaria agreed. "It looks pretty different from the auroras we have on Zix. Although, I actually don't know that much about them on my planet, either."

Jax was pleased to hear that. "We have two types of auroras on Earth. One at each pole. In the north, they're called the *Aurora Borealis*. The word aurora came from the ancient Roman goddess of the dawn and borealis came from the Greek word for wind of the north. They're also nicknamed the Northern Lights."

"So, auroras have been observed for a long time?" Zaria asked.

"Uh-huh." Jax replied. "In the south, they're called *Aurora Australis*. Those are also called the Southern Lights."

"Makes sense," Zaria said. "But what causes them?"

Aurora Borealis seen from Yukon Territory, Canada

Jax said, "In our solar system, they're caused by the Sun. The Sun sends out charged particles called *plasma* that are too small to see. The particles stream toward the Earth in what is called a *solar wind*. They move really fast—a million miles per hour. That's over 1,600,000 kilometers per hour. But even at that rate, it still takes them about 40 hours to reach our atmosphere."

"What happens when they reach the Earth's atmosphere?" Zaria asked.

"Watch!" Jax used his phone to show Zaria a video of an aurora moving. He explained, "They collide with gases that are in our atmosphere, like oxygen and nitrogen. That's when we see those bands of colors. It's similar to what happens inside a neon sign—though I don't know if you have those on Zix."

Zaria looked at a picture of a neon sign that Jax showed her on his phone. "Not exactly, although I think we do have lights that work in a similar way. But the lights from the aurora on Earth are so beautiful. What makes them swirl around? They look like they're dancing."

"They move because they are following the Earth's magnetic field," Jax said.

"That's awesome!" Zaria was amazed. "So, do the atoms of oxygen and nitrogen make the different colors?"

"I was just reading about that," Jax said. "The colors depend on which gases are involved and how high they are in the atmosphere when they collide with the plasma particles.

Green is the color we see most often. Blue is the rarest. In between, you can see red, orange, yellow, and purple or violet auroras."

You may need a special camera to see blue or purple auroras.

Zaria asked, "What causes the green color?"

"Green comes from oxygen at lower altitudes. But if the oxygen is higher in the atmosphere, that causes a red color."

"That's wild!" Zaria said. "Red and green are so different but they both come from oxygen atoms?"

"Yup." Jax said. "Same thing with nitrogen. At lower altitudes, nitrogen will cause blue auroras. At higher altitudes, purple." Jax paused and then said,

"Another thing that is really cool is that because of the height of their orbit, the astronauts on the International Space Station see auroras from the side."

"Fascinating!" Zaria said. Then she added, "I have more questions."

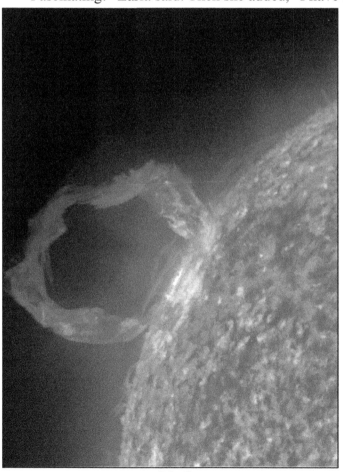

Solar flare

"Go for it!" Jax replied. He liked being able to tell Zaria about things he enjoyed.

"When can you see an aurora? I mean, I realize it would have to be dark out, but are some times better than others?" Zaria asked.

Jax said, "You can't really predict too far in advance when an aurora will happen. They are most likely to be visible in the winter, within a few hours after midnight. But here's where it gets interesting. Our Sun actually has weather. The Sun's weather has a lot to do with auroras."

Zaria asked, "What kind of weather does your Sun have? The stars that our planet Zix revolve around aren't as interesting as your Sun. I think your Sun must be younger and more active than our stars."

Jax explained, "Our Sun has an atmosphere and that's what produces its weather. It has storms. Not like when it rains here on Earth, but when there's a storm on the Sun, it might send out a *coronal mass ejection* or CME for short."

"Does that have something to do with the plasma particles?" Zaria asked.

"Yes." Jax said. "A CME is like a huge bubble of electrified gas that often happens during *solar flares,* when there are huge flashes of light from the surface of the Sun. The CMEs cause *geomagnetic storms* on Earth and can mess up satellite, TV, and radio communications. But the good thing about CMEs is that when they happen, auroras can be seen further away from the poles of the Earth."

"I wish we had such bright light shows on my planet. Ours aren't anywhere near as exciting as yours," Zaria said. "I'd really like to see an aurora here on Earth. Where are the best places to see them?"

Jax said, "You need to be away from the lights of a city to see them. The Aurora Borealis can be easier for people to see than the Aurora Australis. That's because near the north pole, there's a lot more land where people live."

Jax got his globe again and pointed. "If you go to Alaska in the United States, Tromso in Norway, or the Kola different. Peninsula in Russia, you can have an excellent chance of seeing auroras. Although, we can see them in plenty of other places in the north if the conditions are right. In the south—unless you go all the way to Antarctica—you have fewer options. But great locations for seeing the Aurora Australis are Tasmania in Australia and Stewart Island in New Zealand."

Like snowflakes, no two auroras are the same. Their patterns and colors are always different.

"Hey, Jax," Zaria said. "Do you realize we've been talking this whole time and you haven't mentioned the three bears even once?!"

Jax laughed. "You got me on that one. Oh! I almost forgot to tell you about *sunspots.* They're an important part of this, too. Sunspots are dark spots on the Sun that are not as hot as the areas around them. Sunspots also can cause magnificent auroras. The thing is, they come and go in cycles over the course of 11 years. The next time we are scheduled for maximum sunspot activity will be in 2024. I hope we see lots of auroras then!"

"What about auroras on other planets in your solar system? Do they have auroras, too?" asked Zaria.

"If a planet has an atmosphere and a magnetic field, it can have auroras." Jax explained. "NASA's Voyager missions, the Hubble Space Telescope, and other satellites have observed auroras above different planets. They've sent back pictures of auroras from Jupiter, Saturn, Uranus, and Neptune."

Sunspots

"Are they as lovely as the ones on Earth?" Zaria asked.

Jax was pleased that Zaria thought the Earth's auroras were so beautiful. "The auroras are even more intense on Jupiter and Saturn. That's because their magnetic fields are larger and more powerful than the Earth's."

Jax was so focused on talking with Zaria that he hadn't been watching the time. He didn't notice when Ollie picked up his head and looked toward the bedroom door.

Suddenly, the bedroom door flew open, and Jax and Zaria heard Jefferson say, "Hey Jax, pizza time! Get your head out of your work and let's… WHAT'S GO-ING ON?!!"

Aurora Activity

To make your own picture of an aurora, try this activity:

You will need:
1. Oil pastels in green, yellow, red, pink, and blue
2. A piece of black construction paper
3. A piece of construction paper in a lighter color
4. Scissors
5. Paper towels

What to do:
1. Cut a wavy edge along the side of the lighter piece of construction paper, like this:

3. Place the wavy edge on the black construction paper, about 1/3 of the way up from the bottom of the black paper. Use one of the pastels to trace the wavy edge on the lighter paper. Press down to get lots of color on the paper. It's OK if some goes on the black paper, too.
4. Use the paper towel to smudge the color upward onto the black construction paper.
5. Repeat with the same color or with other colors.
6. Move the guide to a different angle, or up or down, to add layers of color to complete your aurora.

Observe:
1. Your aurora illustration!

* see https://spaceplace.nasa.gov/pastel-aurora/en/ for details about this activity

Chapter 8 – Stellar Nurseries and Doggie Alien Sitting

"Oh no. Uh…hey..." Jax said. "Zaria, meet my best friend, Jeff."

Jeff was sputtering, "Is…is that…it…she…."

"An alien?" Jax finished for him. "Yep."

"Hello, Jeff!" Zaria said. "I've heard a bit about you. I'm Zaria from the planet Zix. Jax and I have been working on our projects together."

Jefferson looked at Jax. "She speaks English?!"

Zaria answered, "Actually, I'm speaking Zixian. You are *hearing* English. It's something beings from Zix can do with any language."

At that, Ollie woofed at Zaria.

"Ollie wants me to tell you that I speak Dog, too," Zaria said with a smile.

"Whoaaa! That's awesome!" Jeff said. "Wait 'til the guys hear about *this*!" Zaria and Jax said together, "NO!"

Jax added, "Sorry, Jeff. I think we need to keep this quiet for a while. I haven't even told my mom or Fish Fart Face about Zaria, yet."

Zaria said, "Who is Fish Fart Face? Is that your sister? Does she look like a fish? And isn't a fart made of gas? Is her face gaseous?"

Jefferson and Jax laughed. "No, her name is Gwen. We just call her Fish Fart Face to annoy her. She calls us 'The Presidents' because there were two presidents in our history named Jackson and Jefferson. She thinks she's being clever but we think it's kind of cool. We'd never tell her that, though. If we did, she'd come up with some names that might really annoy us."

"I've been studying your planet for a while, but it seems I still have a lot to learn about Earthlings!" Zaria sighed.

"So, why are you visiting Jax, Zaria? You said you have a project?" Jeff asked.

"On Zix, we have something called Zorketh training. That's where we learn about things in space and space travel. I have to complete a project for that by learning three things about Earth, and I located Jax to help." Zaria answered

Jeff looked at Jax. "Can Zaria come out with us for pizza? That would show her more about Earth. Maybe she could come along on your phone."

"We should keep this quiet for now," Jax replied. He looked at Zaria. "I think it's best to keep things the way they are. Except we'll be working with Jeff, too, if that's OK."

"OK? That's great!" Zaria said. "And I understand about not coming along with you. But I hope we can do that someday."

"Me, too. Well, we have to go to dinner now." Jax said.

"Will Jeff be returning with you?" Zaria asked.

"I don't think anything would keep him away! He can stay over tonight if it's OK with his parents," Jax said.

"I'm sure it'll be fine," Jeff nodded enthusiastically. "See you later, Zaria."

Once Jax and Jeff had gone, Zaria looked at Ollie and said, "I guess it's just you and me for a while, Ollie."

Ollie woofed. "Hey, Zaria, I have a question for you. Do you have dogs on Zix?"

"Sorry, Ollie. We don't. We have pets that look kind of like Earthling cats, only larger. They're called ziaphurs. My ziaphur is fluffy and mostly green with a blue and green striped tail and yellow paws. Her name is 'Zutter' and she is very sweet. I think you'd like her." Zaria paused and then said, "You don't look very impressed, Ollie."

Ollie woofed a small sigh. "Oh, well. If I go to Zix with Jax someday, I guess I'll just have to make friends with Zutter."

"That's the spirit!" Zaria said cheerfully. "I'm going to work on my notes about auroras now. Give a woof when you hear Jax and Jeff coming back, and I'll be ready to tell them about stellar nurseries."

Before long, Ollie woofed. Jax and Jeff were back, and Jeff had his overnight bag. "We're here, Zaria!" Jax said. "I brought Jeff up to speed on what we're doing. He's going to listen in on stellar nurseries and then he'll help me tell you about hurricanes."

"What about Jeff's project?" Zaria asked.

"He's worked a lot on his already," Jax explained. "And he can use some of what we talk about for stellar nurseries for the last part of his project."

"Perfect!" Zaria said. "OK, I'll show you a sped-up time lapse of a *stellar nursery* in action, and then we can talk about it."

Stellar nursery

Jeff was practically bouncing with anticipation, "This is SO awesome!"

"Just wait, Jeff," Jax said. "This is gonna be great!"

"Watch the ceiling. Here we go." Zaria said.

As the room darkened, Jeff and Jax could make out a large, fuzzy, fluffy cloud on the ceiling. Suddenly, it collapsed inward and then seemed to ignite and form a star.

"That's the coolest thing I've ever seen," Jeff said.

Jax nodded in agreement. "Zaria, please tell us what we just saw!"

Zaria laughed and said, "That was the birth of a star. Stars have a kind of life cycle. They begin their life cycle in a *nebula*."

"We talked about those when we were talking about supernovas," Jax said. "They are clouds of dust and gases, right?"

"Right." Zaria was pleased that Jax remembered. "Do you remember what the gases in a nebula are?"

"Mostly hydrogen and helium," Jax said.

Jeff was impressed. "You've learned a lot!"

"Well, Zaria makes things easy to understand," Jax said.

"You're not bad at that, either, Jax," Zaria added. "But let me tell you a bit more about nebulas. They come in many sizes, but mostly they're pretty huge. It can be a lot of light years from one end of a nebula to the other.

"Wait, what's a light year?" Jeff asked.

"Sorry, Jeff, we talked about that before you got here. A light year is the distance that light travels in a year. That's about 6 trillion miles or a little less than 10 trillion kilometers," Zaria replied. "Jax and I also talked about it as traveling at about 186,000 miles per second, or 300,000 kilometers per second."

Zaria continued, "About 1500 light years away from here, there's a nebula with a lot of star formation going on. It's in the part of your sky known as the constellation Orion. Earthlings call it the Orion Nebula. It's a great place to learn how stars are born. Nebulas are pretty distinctive looking. I think they're beautiful, too."

Think about what clouds on Earth are made of. Why can't they form new stars?

"But what we saw was only one star being formed. Why are they called stellar nurseries?" Jax asked.

"That's because typically, many stars are formed within a nebula. They don't always form the same way, though. There are three main categories of nebulas where stars can be formed," Zaria said.

"The three bears!" Jax exclaimed. "I knew we'd get back to them eventually!"

"What?" Jeff asked.

"Don't ask!" Zaria said with a smile. "Seems that a lot of things we've talked about have three main categories, and Jax keeps wanting to relate them to the three bears. Problem is, that's not a story we know on Zix."

"I can tell you the story," Jeff offered.

"OK, but later," Zaria laughed. "I can see that my education about Earth will not be complete until one of you tells me that story!"

"What are the types of nebulas?" Jax said, bringing the discussion back to stellar nurseries.

"The first is called an *emission nebula*," Zaria said. "An emission nebula gets formed when gas and dust in the *interstellar medium* eventually collapse."

Jeff asked, "What's the interstellar medium?"

Zaria explained, "As much as it might look like the areas in galaxies between stars and planets are just empty space, there's actually gas, dust, and cosmic rays in those spaces. That's the interstellar medium."

Orion

"But why do the gas and dust collapse?" Jax asked.

Zaria thought for a moment. "They collapse under their own weight. When that happens, the dust and gas get crushed together and get really, really hot. Then, the hydrogen ignites. That forms a new star. A star like your Sun can take about a million years to form."

"Does a nebula form stars one at a time?" Jax wanted to know.

"No, lots of stars can be formed simultaneously in a nebula. Larger stars are usually created in the center of the region. Those shoot out ultraviolet radiation that often glows in a color you might see as red or pink. The color is from the hydrogen gas."

Jeff said, "Cool! Sounds like a light sabre!"

The coldest known object in our Universe is the Boomerang Nebula. It is − 458°F (272° C) and looks like an hourglass or bow tie.

Zaria laughed. "I don't know what a light sabre is, Jeff! I think of it as more like a laser beam or a giant light bulb. They can really light up the nebula."

"Can we see one from Earth?" Jeff asked.

"Yes." Zaria replied. "You can see an emission nebula in Orion. You don't even need a telescope to see it. You can use a smaller piece of equipment. I think Earthlings call them binoculars. All you need to do is look below and to the right of those three bright stars in a row that are known as Orion's Belt. You'll see a vertical row of what look like stars that form Orion's sword. But the fuzzy-looking thing that looks like a star in the middle of the sword is actually the nebula I mentioned, the Orion Nebula."

Jax said, "If it's clear later tonight, let's look for it."

Zaria and Jeff said together, "Definitely!"

"For now, though, let's talk about the second main type of nebula," Zaria suggested. "It's called a *reflection nebula* because it doesn't have enough energy to ignite its hydrogen atoms and create its own light. It shines because it reflects light from stars that are nearby. New stars are formed in the brightest part of a reflection nebula."

"Cool!" Jax said. "Are they red and pink, too?"

"Newborn stars in reflection nebulas are more likely to look blue to human eyes," Zaria said. "That's because the blue light of the new stars gets scattered more easily than the other colors as it bounces off the dust in the nebula. The same thing explains why the Earth's sky looks blue during the day. There are other colors in your sky, but they mostly pass through the atmosphere without being reflected. At sunrise or sunset, the path of the light changes. That's when you might see beautiful red or orange or yellow colors."

"This is amazing. I never knew that!" Jeff said.

"Where can we see a reflection nebula?" Jax asked.

"Well, you'll need a telescope, but there's one near the supergiant star Rigel, which is also in Orion. Humans call it the Witchhead Nebula," said Zaria as the ceiling changed to show an image of it.

"It looks like the profile of a wicked witch with a hooked nose and a pointy chin!" exclaimed Jeff.

Witchhead Nebula

"It does, Jeff. Hey, maybe your dad will help us find it with his telescope," Jax said.

"I'm sure he would!" Jeff eagerly replied. "What's the third main type of nebula, Zaria?"

"The third category is a *dark nebula*," Zaria said. "Dark nebulas are so dense that they block out anything behind them. They don't reflect light and they don't give off light. They look like a dark area in space. Remember, nebulas are huge, so a dark nebula can even hide a galaxy that might be behind it."

"A whole galaxy? Wow! But why are they so dark?" Jeff asked.

"Interesting question! The dust particles that are in a dark nebula are tiny but they are covered with molecules that block any visible light. It's the bright lights of stars and galaxies that shine around dark nebulas that allow us to see them."

"Are they still stellar nurseries?" Jax asked.

Zaria said, "Yes. And like other types of nebulas, in addition to stars, dark nebulas can also give birth to planets and moons. There's a dark nebula in Orion that you call the Horsehead Nebula." Once again, the ceiling changed to show a view of the nebula.

"It looks like a horse's head poking up into space!" exclaimed Jeff.

"Orion is one busy constellation." Jax observed.

"It is, but it's actually hard to see the Horsehead Nebula with just a small telescope. If you're fortunate, you can find it just south of Alnitak, the star that is on the left end of Orion's belt," Zaria said.

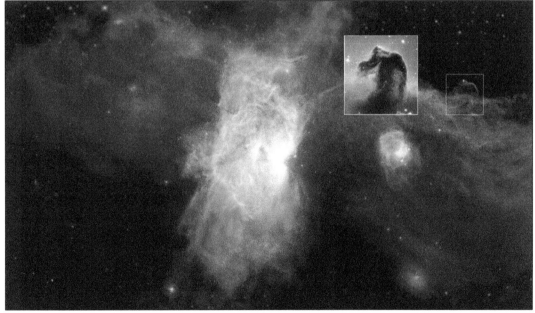

Horsehead Nebula

"Zaria, I have another question. You mentioned that stars have a type of life cycle," Jax said. "What happens at the end of a star's life?"

Zaria said, "Well, remember, we talked about how when a star runs out of fuel, it can become a red supergiant star and then a supernova. If the star doesn't have enough mass to become a supernova, it can form a *planetary nebula* before becoming a white dwarf."

"What's a planetary nebula?" Jeff asked.

"A planetary nebula is a type of emission nebula. So, the cycle of star formation can begin again. That's why it's like a life cycle.

"Which will happen to our Sun? Will it go supernova or turn into a white dwarf?" Jeff asked.

"Your Sun isn't massive enough to explode as a supernova. It will puff off its outer layers as a planetary nebula before turning into a white dwarf – but not for about five billion years." Zaria said.

Helix Nebula

Jax asked, "Is there a planetary nebula we could see now?"

"Sure!" Zaria replied. "The closest planetary nebula to the Earth is called the Helix Nebula in your constellation Aquarius. You can see it with a good pair of binoculars. Or, you might use your dad's telescope to look for the planetary nebula called the Cat's Eye Nebula.

Suddenly, Clara called out, "Jeff! Jax! Time for a bedtime snack if you want one and then lights out."

"Be there in a sec, Mom!" Jax called out. "We have to call it a night, Zaria."

Ollie woofed.

"I didn't forget, Ollie." Zaria said. "Ollie asked if he could have extra treats tonight for having been such a good alien sitter while you went out to eat pizza."

"OK, Ollie, but I'm not sure Zaria appreciates the idea of you as her alien sitter." Jax said.

"It was fun," Zaria said. "I like talking with Ollie."

Ollie woofed and Zaria smiled.

"Where will you go while we sleep?" Jeff asked.

Zaria replied, "I'll be home. In Zix time, I've only been gone a twinkle but my family would worry if I were gone too long."

"C'mon Jeff. See you tomorrow, Zaria!" Jax said,

"I'll be ready to hear about hurricanes!" Zaria said just before disappearing from the laptop screen.

Stellar Nurseries Activity

You will need:
1. Colored, metallic confetti
2. A piece of thick, black construction paper or cardboard, cut into an interesting shape
3. A flashlight

What to do:
1. To get an idea of what a reflection nebula looks like, throw some metallic confetti into the air in a dark room (or better yet, outside at night so you don't make a mess!).
2. Shine a flashlight onto the confetti.
3. To get an idea of what a dark nebula looks like, in a dark room set up a piece of black construction paper or cardboard and shine a flashlight behind it.

Observe:
1. With the confetti, you will see the colored lights reflected, like with a reflection nebula.
2. The construction paper or cardboard will block the light from shining through it but you will be able to see the edges of the shape of the paper or cardboard, like with a dark nebula.

Chapter 9 – Hurricanes and THAD

Jefferson poked Jax on the arm. "Jax, wake up!"

"What time is it?" Jax asked.

"It's 5:30. The sun's coming up!" Jeff couldn't contain his enthusiasm.

"5:30?! Are you crazy?! Go back to sleep." Jax mumbled.

Jeff was insistent, "Wake up, dude! I want to see if Zaria is back."

Jax opened one eye and looked at Jeff. "You're already dressed? OK, give me a minute."

Jax returned from the bathroom, threw on some jeans and a shirt, and turned on his laptop. Zaria instantly came on the screen.

"Hi Zaria!" Jeff said cheerfully. "I had to wake Jax up. I thought he was going to sleep until noon!"

"It must be early on Earth," Zaria observed. "Ollie isn't even awake yet."

"Ollie might have more sense than some people." Jax said with a smile. "Well, are you ready for hurricanes?"

Zaria smiled, "I sure am!"

"Be right back." Jax said as he started looking in his closet again. "I knew I'd saved it! Here is my model of a hurricane that I did for a science project for school."

"You sure do neat things in your school," Zaria observed.

"I guess we do!" Jax thought for a moment. "Hmmm… This time let's save the demonstration. I think it'll make more sense after we talk about hurricanes a bit."

Zaria said, "Sounds good."

Jeff started by saying, "Hurricanes are really huge storms that are most likely to happen in our area in late summer. They can come one after another."

"Right." Jax said. "And they are called by different names. What they are called depends on where they happen. The generic name for hurricanes is *tropical cyclones*." He picked up his globe and pointed. "In North America and in the Caribbean, they are called *hurricanes*. In the South Pacific and Indian Ocean, they are known as *cyclones*. And in Southeast Asia, they are called *typhoons*."

Storm surge

"I guess that's too many names to have for the three bears," Zaria laughed.

"True! For now, we'll just call them all hurricanes, OK?" Jax asked. "No matter what they're called, they're one of the most powerful storms on Earth."

Jeff added, "Lots of hurricanes happen out in the oceans and don't hit land. When they hit land, though, they can last a week or more. And they can cause a lot of damage."

"That's for sure." Jax agreed. "That's because hurricanes have fierce winds and can have huge amounts of rain. They can cause *storm surges*, giant waves, and flooding. They can even set off *tornadoes*."

"I know that a tornado is one of those storms that looks like a rotating funnel. But what's a storm surge?" Zaria asked.

Jeff answered, "Storm surges are what can happen when a hurricane hits land. It's when the level of the ocean gets really, really high at the coastline."

Did you ever do a "cannonball" jump into a pool? How is that like a storm surge?

"I think we're getting ahead of ourselves," Jax said. "Let's talk about how hurricanes form."

"Seems like a good place to begin." Zaria agreed.

"Hurricanes form over warm ocean water. They begin near the *Equator*," Jax said, pointing to the Equator's line around the center of his globe. "Hurricanes also need wind to develop. As the wind passes over the warm water, it takes the water with it."

Zaria interrupted, "Where does it go?"

"Well," Jax took a deep breath. "This is what happens. The wind whips the water upward. The air is warm and so the water it takes *evaporates*. That means that it becomes a gas. The air becomes very moist. As it rises, the water that had evaporated cools down and it starts to *condense*. That means that it becomes liquid again. Then, droplets form that build into a large storm cloud."

"Is that when it becomes a hurricane?" Zaria asked.

"Not yet," Jax replied. "As the droplets form the storm cloud, heat is released. As the heat is released, the *air pressure* – the weight of the air - near the top of the storm cloud increases. It pushes the wind outward."

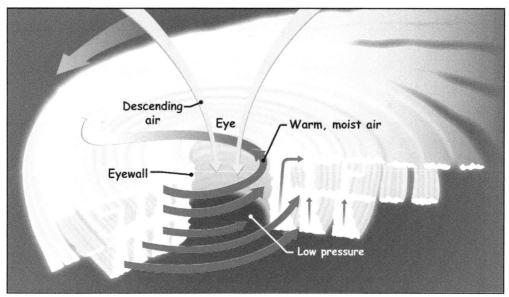

Diagram of air pressure movement in a hurricane

"Is that the wind that makes the hurricane?" Zaria interrupted.

"Not yet," Jax smiled. "It's kinda complicated. The thing is, the activity at the surface of the water causes the air pressure down there to decrease. So, the cooler air at the top of the storm cloud drops to even out the air pressure."

Jeff picked up the explanation. "Imagine that happening over and over. The storm cloud gets bigger and higher as it builds until it becomes a cluster of thunderstorm clouds. Then, the winds start to rotate around the center of the storm cloud. At that point, it's called a *tropical disturbance*."

"Sounds dramatic." Zaria said. "But what makes it finally become a hurricane?"

"It depends on the speed of the winds," Jax said. "If the winds are between 25 and 38 miles per hour – that's about 40 to 61 kilometers per hour – it becomes a *tropical depression*. Once the winds get to 39 miles per hour – that's about 63 kilometers per hour – it's a *tropical storm*. The winds have to reach 74 miles per hour – that's almost 120 kilometers per hour – to become a hurricane."

Jeff jumped in, "At that point, it's enormous. The *height* of the clouds is at least 50,000 feet. That's 15,000 meters. The *diameter*, the distance across the clouds, is at least 125 miles. That's over 200 kilometers."

Jax picked up the globe. "That's almost the distance from New York City to Philadelphia. And just in case that sounds like a lot, the diameter can be over 600 miles. That's almost 1,000 kilometers. That's close to the distance from Rome in Italy to Frankfurt in Germany!"

"And as the hurricane moves toward land, it swirls around its *eye*," Jeff said. "The eye is at the center of the hurricane. In the eye, the winds are calm. Typically, there are no clouds. The eye is huge, too. It can be from 5 to 30 miles—or 8 to about 48 kilometers—across."

"But watch out!" Jax said. "The *eye wall* is a super dangerous part of a hurricane. The eye wall is at the edge of the eye. That's where the winds reach their highest speeds."

Zaria smiled, "You two are amazing teachers! I really like how you go back and forth with all this information."

Hurricane Isaac

"Thanks, Zaria," Jeff smiled back. "It's helpful that Jax and I did a big project together about hurricanes for science class."

Jax was very pleased, too. "Wait 'til you hear this, Zaria. In the *Northern Hemisphere*, which is above the Equator, hurricanes spin in a counter-clockwise direction. That's like going backwards around a clock, from west to east. But in the *Southern Hemisphere*, which is below the Equator, they spin in a clockwise direction, from east to west. That's like going the right way around a clock."

How can a bulldozer be like a hurricane?

"Why?" Zaria asked.

Eye of the storm

"It's because of the rotation of the Earth," Jax replied. "It's called the *Coriolis Effect*."

"That's cool!" Zaria said. "I'm guessing that the speed of the wind has something to do with the damage that a hurricane can cause. Is that right?"

"Absolutely." Jeff answered. "In fact, hurricanes are given a number from 1 to 5 based on their wind speed. The higher the number, the more damage they can create when they hit land. A category 1 hurricane has winds between 74 and 95 miles per hour. That's about 120 to just over 150 kilometers per hour. A category 5 hurricane has winds of 157 miles per hour or higher. That's over 250 kilometers per hour."

Jeff added, "The numbers are also identified with labels. The labels go from minimal to moderate, extensive, extreme, and catastrophic. Fortunately, category 5—catastrophic hurricanes—don't happen too often."

Jax continued, "Usually, though, a hurricane gets weaker when it hits land. That's because it loses the energy it gets from the warm ocean water. It can also weaken if it moves north where the land or the ocean water is cooler."

"We have to tell Zaria about naming hurricanes," Jeff said.

"Hurricanes have names?" Zaria exclaimed. "Like Jackson? Or Jefferson? Or Ollie?"

Hearing his name, Ollie opened one eye and woofed to Zaria.

"Ollie would like his breakfast treats," Zaria interpreted.

Jax pretended to scold Ollie. "Breakfast treats?! Ollie, you know you don't eat treats for breakfast. C'mon. We'll go for a quick walk and then get your dog food."

Ollie woofed again.

Zaria translated, "And some treats, please, for being such a good boy."

Jax laughed. "OK, but don't I always give you a treat after your walk?!"

Then Jax said, "I'll be right back. Jeff, will you tell Zaria about naming hurricanes while I'm out with Ollie?"

You might like looking up other hurricane names used around the world

Jeff said, "Sure, no problem! Here's what happens, Zaria. Naming practices vary. For the Atlantic Ocean, the World Meteorological Organization uses six lists of names that get rotated. Each year starts with a new list. Each list always starts with a name that begins with an A. Names that start with Q, U, X, Y, and Z are not on the lists. That's because the Atlantic region doesn't have a lot of names that begin with those letters."

"So, there won't be a Hurricane Zaria," Zaria sighed.

"No...sorry!" Jeff said. "There could be a Hurricane Jeff, though, because names alternate between male and female names. That's both for the names on the list and whether the list starts with a female or male name. It wasn't always like that, though. Hurricanes used to have only female names."

"What happens if the whole list is used up in a year?" Zaria asked.

Jeff said, "That usually doesn't happen, but for the Atlantic Ocean, the Greek Alphabet letters would be used. So, we'd have Hurricane Alpha, Hurricane Beta, and so on."

"If a hurricane is really bad," Jeff continued, "the name that it was given is retired. That means that the name is taken off of its list forever. It gets replaced with a name that starts with the same letter. In 2005, there was a truly catastrophic category 5 hurricane named Katrina. The name Katrina was retired. It was replaced with the name Katia."

Just then, Jax returned with Ollie close behind. He reached into Ollie's treat jar and said, "Here you go, Ollie. Tell Zaria you were a good boy!"

Ollie woofed and Zaria woofed back at him.

Hurricane Katrina

"I told him that I'm proud of him for being a good boy," Zaria said. "Hey, I just thought of another question. It sounds like hurricanes can be very dangerous. Is there a way to predict them or which way they will go?"

Jax replied, "There's more and more sophisticated information each year to help with that. It comes from many agencies including NOAA, which is the National Oceanic and Atmospheric Administration, NASA, and groups in Europe. They have satellites, special planes, and computer models and animations that do a good job of predicting and studying hurricanes."

"What about hurricanes on other planets in the solar system?" Zaria asked.

"We're learning about those, too. Some good information came in from NASA's Cassini Spacecraft before it dove into Saturn at the end of its mission," Jax said.

"Jupiter and Saturn have storms that are bigger and more violent than the hurricanes on Earth," Jeff said. "It might be because the winds on those planets are stronger than the winds we have here."

Jax said, "On Jupiter, the *Great Red Spot* is a giant spinning storm that has been raging for over 180 years. It's so big that it could fit two Earths inside it."

"And Saturn's *Great White Spot* is a huge storm with lightning that is stronger than any we have on Earth. Its winds have been observed at as much as 330 miles per hour. That's 530 kilometers an hour. And its eye is gigantic. It's about 1,250 miles across. That's over 2,000 kilometers," Jeff added.

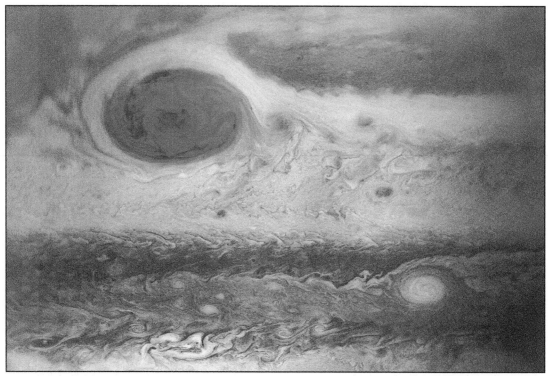

Jupiter

"Another interesting thing about Saturn's Great White Spot is that it isn't always there. It comes and goes every 20-30 Earth years," Jax said.

Jeff said, "Don't forget Neptune. Neptune has the strongest winds in our solar system. It has a storm on its south pole that also seems to come and go. It's called the *Great Dark Spot*. That's because it looks like a dark oval."

"Guess we'll have to be careful of hurricanes no matter where we travel," Zaria said. "I think I'm ready for that demonstration now, Jax."

"OK!" Jax said.

Jax took two plastic soft drink bottles and filled the bottom one about ¾ of the way with water. He taped the two mouths of the bottles together and then swirled the bottles around. Then, he flipped the bottles over. The water spun like a whirlpool into the empty bottle that was now on the bottom.

"That was really cool!" Zaria said. "Though, why do you look so sad, Jax?"

Jax smiled, "Well, this has been so much fun. But I just realized that we have all the information for my project and for your Zorketh training, too. I guess I'm bummed out that we're finished."

"Oh, but we'll get together again!" Zaria assured him. "Let's meet in about three Earth weeks. I'll know whether I've passed my Zorketh training level by then."

Saturn

"And we should have our grades on our projects, too." Jax replied, feeling cheerful again. "So…in three weeks, Jeff can sleep over again and we'll meet and compare how we did!"

"Yay!" Jeff couldn't help shouting.

Ollie woofed.

"Of course you're invited, Ollie! We wouldn't be Team Human Alien Dog without you!" Zaria said.

"Team Human Alien Dog—THAD—that's us!" Jeff said. "Until three weeks when THAD meets again!"

"Three weeks!" Zaria echoed as she waved goodbye and disappeared from Jax's laptop screen.

"Did that really just happen?" Jeff asked.

"It did," Jax answered. And he knew the next three weeks were going to feel like the longest three weeks in his life.

Hurricane Activity

You will need:
1. Two large empty plastic soft drink bottles
2. Some glitter, food coloring, or sand (all optional but they help to see the effect)
3. Water
4. Duct tape

What to do:
1. Put some glitter, food coloring, and/or sand in one of the soft drink bottles.
2. Fill that bottle about ¾ of the way with water.
3. Use the duct tape to tightly tape the mouths of the two bottles together. Try your best to make it watertight. You may need to tape up a bit from both mouths to do that.
4. Holding the bottle with the water, swirl the bottles with a circular motion.
5. Quickly turn the bottles over so the empty bottle is on the bottom.

Observe:
1. The water will swirl around the neck of the bottle while the air moves quickly up through the center. It will look like a whirlwind.
2. Notice what happens to the glitter, food coloring, and/or sand as they move through the "hurricane."

Chapter 10 – Good Grades and New Beginnings

"Ready for chocolate cake?" Clara asked.

Jax, Jeff, and Gwen all yelled, "YES!"

Clara brought the cake, a knife, plates, and forks to the table. The top of the cake looked like this:

"I'm proud of you, Jax," Gwen said. "You did very well. Congratulations!"

"Thanks, Gwen!" Jax said. He was so happy that he didn't even feel like calling her Fish Fart Face. After all, not only did he and Jeff each get an A+ on their projects, tonight was the night that they were going to see Zaria again. He hoped that she'd passed her Zorketh training. Otherwise, the celebration wouldn't be complete.

Just as Jax was thinking that it was too bad that Zaria couldn't have some of his mom's delicious chocolate cake, Jeff exclaimed, "This is the best cake ever, Mrs. Bishop!" It was like Jeff had read Jax's mind.

"Thanks, Jeff. I'm glad you like it." Clara said. "So, are you ready for the final game in your soccer tournament?"

"I hope so. Are you coming to the game, Mrs. B.?" Jeff asked.

Clara replied, "I wouldn't miss it! Your team has worked so hard all season. No matter what happens, it's great that you made it to the final. Although, I hope you win the trophy."

"If we do," Jeff asked, "will you make another cake like this?"

"You bet!" Clara replied, laughing. "I'll make one even if you don't win. We'll either celebrate or drown our disappointment with chocolate cake!"

"You're the best, Mrs. B!" Jeff said through a mouth full of cake.

"I won't tell your mom that you said that!" laughed Clara.

"She's the best, too. Just not at making chocolate cake," Jeff quickly said.

"Nice save, Jeff," Gwen smiled.

After everyone helped clean up the dishes, Jeff, Jax, and Ollie headed toward Jax's room. "C'mon, Ollie. You can have a celebration treat, too," Jax said.

Ollie didn't need to hear the word "treat" twice. He was the first one to get to Jax's room.

Jax closed the door and then turned on his laptop, while Jeff gave Ollie a treat. Zaria was there, waiting for them.

"I call to order an official meeting of THAD!" she said. "The first order of business is, how did you do on your projects?"

"A+! The best we could get!" Jeff and Jax called out at the same time.

Zaria laughed. "That's great! GO THAD!"

"How about you, Zaria? Did you pass your Zorketh training?" asked Jax.

Zaria broke out in a big smile. "Not only did I pass and advance to the next Zorketh level, I did so well that I was awarded an extra ability!"

"What does that mean?" Jeff asked.

Suddenly, Zaria seemed to dissolve into small twinkling lights. And then the laptop screen went dark.

"Oh, no." Jax moaned. "What a time to have laptop problems."

Ollie woofed toward the corner of Jax's room. There, the twinkling lights seemed to be reassembling.

"You don't have laptop problems at all, Jax," said a voice that sounded like Zaria, only it was coming from the lights. "This is my new ability!"

And with that, Zaria appeared, standing in Jax's room.

Not a computer image.

Not a hologram.

A real, live girl from Zix.

Words to Know

Active Volcano – a volcano that has erupted and is likely to erupt again.

Air pressure – the weight of the air as it presses down on the surface of the Earth.

Ash Cloud – Bits of burnt rock from a volcano that can form a cloud and enter the Earth's atmosphere.

Atom –a tiny particle that is the building block for matter, which combines to form molecules.

Aurora Australis – Also called the Southern Lights. Bands of light in the southern pole area that are caused by solar particles interacting with gases in the Earth's atmosphere that follow the Earth's magnetic lines of force.

Aurora Borealis – Also called the Northern Lights. Bands of light in the northern pole area that are caused by solar particles interacting with gases in the Earth's atmosphere that follow the Earth's magnetic lines of force.

Binary Star System – Two stars that orbit around each other, such as a white dwarf star with a companion star in a Type I supernova.

Black Hole – an area in space that has so much gravitational pull that even light cannot get out.

Caldera – a large crater at the top of a volcano.

Cinder Cone Volcano – a volcano shaped like a cone but not very tall.

Composite volcano – a volcano shaped like a cone or mountain that has been formed by lava built up over many years and can be very tall.

Companion Star – a star paired with a white dwarf in a Type I supernova.

Condense – a process where water vapor cools and becomes liquid again.

Coriolis Effect – the name given to how the rotation of the Earth causes hurricanes to spin counter-clockwise in the Northern Hemisphere and clockwise in the Southern Hemisphere.

Coronal Mass Ejection (CME) – a gigantic cloud of solar plasma that is sent at high speed out from the Sun during a solar flare.

Cyclone – a hurricane that occurs in the South Pacific and Indian Ocean.

Dark Nebula – a nebula with a cloud that is so dense that it blocks out what is behind it and looks like a dark area in space.

Diameter of a Hurricane – the distance from one side of a hurricane to the other side.

Dormant volcano – a volcano that has erupted but is not expected to erupt again soon.

Earth's Crust – Top layer of the Earth.

Emission Nebula – a type of nebula where stars are formed by the collapse of gasses in the Interstellar Medium.

Equator – the imaginary line around the center of the Earth that separates the Earth into the Northern and Southern Hemispheres.

Evaporate – when water is warmed and becomes a vapor or a gas.

Event Horizon – the point of no return for a black hole. Matter that crosses over the event horizon falls into the black hole.

Extinct Volcano – a volcano that is unlikely to erupt again.

Fault Lines –cracks in the Earth's crust.

Eye of a Hurricane – the center of a hurricane, which is usually calm.

Eye Wall – a dangerous part of a hurricane at the edge of the eye, where winds can reach their highest speeds.

Geomagnetic Storm – solar wind that causes a disturbance in the magnetosphere around the Earth.

Gravity – the force that attracts two objects toward each other. For example, gravity keeps you on Earth.

Great Dark Spot – hurricane-like storm on Neptune.

Great Red Spot – hurricane-like storm on Jupiter.

Great White Spot – hurricane-like storm on Saturn.

Height of a Hurricane – measurement of how tall a hurricane is.

Hurricane – one of the fiercest storms on Earth.

Interstellar Medium – gases, dust, and cosmic rays between planets and stars in a galaxy.

Lava – hot liquid that has been hurled out of a volcano.

Lava Dome Volcano - a volcano formed when lava is too thick to flow and builds up on the side of a volcano.

Light year - how far light can travel in a year: about 186,000 miles per second, or 300,000 kilometers per second.

Magma – hot liquid inside a volcano.

Mantle (Earth)– Middle layer of the Earth.

Mass – the amount of matter in an object.

Nebula (plural is **Nebulas** or **Nebulae**) – A cloud of dust and gas in the Interstellar Medium.

Neutron Star – the core of a collapsed star that exploded as a supernova.

Northern Hemisphere – the half of the Earth that is above the Equator.

Pillow Lava – lava from underwater volcanoes that forms pillow shapes.

Planetary Nebula – nebula formed at the end of a star's life.

Plasma – Particles that are too small to see. When sent out from the Sun, plasmas cause auroras when they interact with gases in the Earth's atmosphere.

Primordial Black Hole – the smallest type of black hole that may or may not exist.

Pumice – a light and porous volcanic rock that can float and is abrasive and rough.

Red Supergiant Star – A star near the end of its life. Some collapse in on themselves prior to becoming a Type II supernova.

Reflection Nebula – A nebula that shines by reflecting light from stars that are nearby rather than by creating its own light.

Ring of Fire – A horseshoe-shaped area around the Pacific Ocean where about 90% of the Earth's volcanoes can be found.

Sagittarius A* (or Sagittarius A-Star or Sgr A*) – the supermassive black hole at the center of the Milky Way Galaxy.

Shield volcano – a volcano that is more flat or shaped like a bowl.

Solar Flares – huge flashes of light from the surface of the Sun.

Solar Wind – plasma particles that stream away from the sun at 1 million miles per hour or over 1,600,000 kilometers per hour and cause auroras.

Southern Hemisphere – the half of the Earth that is below the Equator.

Spaghettification – how a star that travels too close to a black hole gets stretched and torn apart.

Stellar Black Holes –black holes resulting from the collapse of a massive star.

Stellar Nurseries – a dense cloud of dust and gas that contracts, ignites, and forms new stars.

Storm Surge – when a hurricane hits land and the level of the ocean rises at the coastline.

Sunspots – dark spots on the Sun that tend to peak in 11-year cycles. They are not as hot as the areas around them. They eject plasma that can create auroras.

Supermassive Black Holes – the largest type of black hole, which can be millions or even billions of times the mass of our Sun, and which reside at the center of most known galaxies.

Supernova - a large star (more massive than our Sun) at the end of its life that collapses, explodes, and blasts parts of itself out into space.

Supernova Remnant – the leftover bits from a supernova that expand outward in every direction.

Tectonic Plates – gigantic portions of the Earth's crust, the top layer of the Earth.

Tornado – a storm with powerful rotating winds that form a column that looks like a funnel from the cloud down toward the ground.

Tropical Cyclone – generic name for a hurricane.

Tropical Depression – when winds reach between 25-38 mph (approximately 40-61 kph) as a hurricane forms.

Tropical Disturbance – a cluster of thunderstorm clouds as a hurricane forms.

Tropical Storm – when winds reach between 39 mph (approximately 63 kph) as a hurricane forms.

Type I (Type 1a) Supernova – type of supernova that needs two stars in what is known as a binary star system.

Type II Supernova – type of supernova that comes from one star that became a red supergiant before exploding.

Typhoon – a hurricane that occurs in Southeast Asia.

Vent – the opening in a volcano.

Volcano – an opening in the surface of a planet or moon that can release material that is warmer than its surroundings.

White Dwarf Star – a star at the end of its life that may take on material from a companion star prior to becoming a Type I supernova.

Image Credits listed by page

About the Authors

Lisa Smith is Professor and Head of the School of Social Sciences at the University of Otago in New Zealand, where she also served as the Dean of the College of Education. After work hours, she turns into "Grammie," her favorite role!

Kimberly Arcand has worked for NASA's Chandra X-ray Observatory for over two decades. She has co-authored five non-fiction popular science books. In her spare time, Kim enjoys spending time with her husband, two kids, and whatever rescue dog she has adopted lately in her home state of Rhode Island (USA, planet Earth)

Grateful acknowledgement goes to the University of Otago for their support.